William Clark Russell

The Tragedy of Ida Noble

A Novel

William Clark Russell

The Tragedy of Ida Noble
A Novel

ISBN/EAN: 9783337032333

Printed in Europe, USA, Canada, Australia, Japan

Cover: Foto ©Andreas Hilbeck / pixelio.de

More available books at **www.hansebooks.com**

THE
TRAGEDY OF IDA NOBLE

A NOVEL

BY
W. CLARK RUSSELL

NEW YORK
D. APPLETON AND COMPANY
1892

CONTENTS.

THE TRAGEDY OF IDA NOBLE.

CHAPTER I.

A YANKEE RUSE.

On Monday, August 8th, 1838, the large bark Ocean Ranger, of which I was second mate, was in latitude 38° 40′ N., and longitude 11° W. The hour was four o'clock in the afternoon. I had come on deck to relieve the chief officer, who had had charge of the ship since twelve. It was a very heavy day—a sullen sky of gray vapor seeming to overhang our mastheads within pistol-shot of the trucks. From time to time there had stolen from the far reaches of the ocean a note as of the groaning of a tempest, but there had been no lightning; the wind hung a steady breeze out of the east, and the ship, with slanting masts and rounded breasts of canvas, showing with a glare of snow against the dark ground of the sky, pushed quietly through

the water that floated in a light swell to the yellow
line of her sheathing.

Some time before I arrived on deck a vessel had
been descried on the port bow, and now at this hour
of four she had risen to the tacks of her courses,
and her sails shone so radiantly in the dusky distance
that at the first glance I knew her to be an American. The captain of my ship, a man named Hoste,
was pacing the deck near the wheel; I trudged the
planks a little way forward of him, stepping athwart-
ships, or from side to side. The men, who were
getting their supper, passed in and out of the galley, carrying hook-pots of steaming tea. It was an
hour of liberty with them, the first of what is
called the " dog watches." The gloom of the sky
seemed to heighten the quietude that was upon the
ship. The sailors talked low, and their laughter
was sudden and short. All was silent aloft, the
sails stirless to the gushing of the long salt breath
of the east wind into the wide spaces of cloths, and
nothing sounded over the side save the dim crackling and soft seething noises of waters broken under
the bow, and sobbing and simmering past, with
now and again a glad note like the fall of a fount-
ain.

The captain picked up a telescope that lay upon

the skylight, and crossing the deck took a view of
the approaching ship; then approached me.

"She is an American," he said.

"Yes, sir."

"How do you know she is an American?"

"By the light of the cotton in her canvas."

"Ay, and there are more signs than that. She
has put her helm over as though she would speak
us."

By five o'clock she was about a mile to a mile
and a quarter distant on our weather bow, at which
hour she had backed her maintop-sail and lay stationary upon the sea, rolling lightly and very stately on the swell, the beautiful flag of her nation—
the stars and stripes—floating inverted from her
peak as a signal of distress. Both Captain Hoste
and I had searched her with a telescope, but we
could see no other signs of life aboard her than three
figures—one of which stood at the wheel—on her
short length of poop, and a single head as of a
sailor viewing us over the bulwark-rail forward.

We shortened sail as we slowly drew down, and
when within speaking distance Captain Hoste
hailed her.

The answer was—"For God's sake send a
boat!" Yet she had good boats of her own, and it

puzzled me, then, that she should request us to send, seeing that there must be hands enough to enable her to back the yards on the main.

Captain Hoste cried out, " But what is wrong with you ? "

One of the figures on the poop or raised deck tossed his hands in a gesture of agitation and distress, and in piteous, nasal Yankee accents repeated, " For God's sake send a boat ! "

Captain Hoste gazed for a while, as though hesitating. He then said to me, " Mr. Portlack, there may be trouble aboard that ship, not to be guessed at by merely looking at her and singing out. Take a couple of hands in the jolly boat and ascertain what is wanted," and so saying he bawled a command to the sailors forward to lay the maintop-sail of the Ocean Ranger to the mast, while I called to others to lay aft and lower away the jolly boat that was suspended at irons called davits, a little distance past the mizzen-rigging.

By this time a darker shade had entered the gloom of the sky, due partly to the sinking of the hidden sun, and partly to the thickening of the atmosphere as for rain. The sea, that ran in folds of leaden hue, was merely wrinkled and crisped by the wind, and I had no difficulty in making head against the streaming foam-lined ripples and in laying the little boat alongside the American.

She was a tall, black ship with an almost straight stem and of a clipper keenness of bow. Her stemhead and quarters were rich with gilt devices; her towering skysail poles, the white trucks of which gleamed like silver, seemed to pierce the dusky surface of vapor above them. I sprang into the mizzen channel and stepped from the rail on to the poop.

Saving the man at the wheel there was but one person on deck; I sent a look forward but the ship was deserted. *This*, I instantly thought to myself, will be a case of mutiny. There has been brutality, or, which is nearly as bad as brutality, bad food, and the men have refused duty and gone below.

The person who received me was an American skipper of a type that travel had rendered familiar. His dress was remarkable for nothing but an immense felt, sugar-loaf-shaped hat—a Fifth of November hat. He had a hard, yellow face with a slight cast in one eye, and his long beard was trimmed to the aspect of a goat's. I did not observe in him any marks of the agitation and distress which had echoed in his melancholy return yell to us of "For God's sake send a boat!" He

eyed me coolly and critically, running his eyes over
me from top to toe as though I were a man soliciting work, and as though he were considering
whether to engage me or not.   He then said,
"Good afternoon!"

"Pray," said I, "what is wrong with you that
you asked us to send a boat?"

"Step below," said he, moving to the little companion hatch that conducted to the cabin.

"I am in a hurry," said I, with a glance round
the sea; "it darkens quickly and I wish to return
to my ship.   Pray let me hear your wants."

"This way, if you please," he answered, putting
his foot upon the ladder.

There was no help for it: I must follow him or
return to my ship without being able to satisfy the
questions which Captain Hoste would put to me.
As I stepped to the hatch it began to rain, but
without increase of wind; away to windward in
the east the sea was already shrouded with drizzle,
and already to leeward the Ocean Ranger loomed
with something of indistinctness in the thickening
atmosphere, her white sails showing in the gathering dusk as she rolled like spaces of pale light flung
and eclipsed, flung and eclipsed again.   The helmsman at the wheel of the Yankee stared hard at me

as I approached the hatch. On entering the cabin, I found the captain with an air of bustle in the act of placing a bottle and glasses upon the table.

"Sit you down, sit you down," he called to me. "Here is such a drop of rum as I know some folks in your country would think cheap at a dollar a glass."

"This is no time to drink," said I, "thanking you all the same, nor is rum a liquor I am accustomed to swallow at this hour. Pray tell me what is wrong with you."

"Wal," said he, "if you won't drink my health, then I just reckon there's nothen for me to do but to drink yourn."

He poured out about a gill of neat rum which, first smelling it, with a noisy smack of his lips he tossed down. I looked at my watch, meaning to give him three minutes and then be off, let his distress be what it might. The cabin was so gloomy that our faces to each other could scarcely be more than a glimmer. The evening shadow, darker yet with rain and with the wet of the rain upon the glass, lay upon the little skylight over the table; the windows overlooking the main deck were narrow apertures, and there was nothing of the ship to be seen through them; yet, even as the Yankee put down his glass, fetching a deep breath as he did so, I seemed to hear a sound as of men softly treading, accompanied by a voice apparently giving orders in subdued tones, and by the noise of rigging carelessly dropped or hastily flung down.

"What ship is yourn?" said the captain.

"The Ocean Ranger," I replied. "But you are trifling with me, I think. I am not here to answer that sort of questions. What do you want?"

"Wal," he answered, "I'll tell you what I want, mister. I'm short of men, and men," he added, with a touch of brutal energy in his tone, "I must have, or, durn me, if the Ephriam Z. Jackson is going to fetch New York this side of Christmas Day. I reckon," he continued, with an indiscribable nasal drawl, "that your captain will be willing to loan me two or three smart hands."

"I reckon," I replied, with some heat, "that he will be willing to do nothing of the sort, if for no other reason than because it's already a tight fit with us in the matter of labor. If *that* is your want—very sorry, I'm sure, that we should be unable to serve you," and I made a step toward the companion ladder.

"Stop, mister," he cried, "how might *you* be rated aboard your ship?"

"Second mate," I replied, pausing and looking round at the man.

"Wal," said he, coolly, "I don't mind telling you that my second mate's little better than a sojer"—by which he meant "soldier"—"and if so be as you are willing to stop just here, I'll break him and send him forrards, where he'll be of some use, and you shall take his place."

My astonishment held me silent for some moments. "Thank you," said I, "my captain is waiting for me to return," and with a stride I gained the companion steps.

"Stop, mister!" he shouted. "Men I must have, and at sea when the pi-rate necessity boards a craft po-liteness has to skip. You can stop if you like; but if you go you goes alone. I tell you I must have men. Two men ye've brought, and they're going to stop, I calculate. *In* fact, we've filled on the Ephriam Z. Jackson, and she's *ony rout* again, mister. If *you* go—"

I stayed to hear no more, and in a bound gained the deck. Sure enough they had swung the topsail yard, and the ship, slowly gathering way, was breaking the wrinkles of the sea which underran her into a little froth under her bows! Five or six sailors were moving about the decks. I rushed to the side to look for my boat; she lay where I had left her, straining at the line, and wobbling and splashing angrily as she was towed; but there was nobody in her. My two men were not to be seen. I shouted their names, my heart beating with alarm and temper, but either they were detained by force below, or, influenced by the seaman's proverbial reckless love of change, they had been swiftly and easily coaxed by a handsome offer of dollars and of rum into skulking out of sight until I should have left the ship. My own vessel lay a mere smudge in the rain away down upon the lee quarter, yet she was not so indistinct but that I was able to make out she had not yet filled on her topsail. I could imagine Captain Hoste bewildered by the action of the Yankee, not yet visited by a suspicion of the fellow's atrocious duplicity, and waiting a while to see what he intended to do.

I had followed the sea for many years, and my profession had taught me speed in forming resolutions. Had the weather been clear, even though the time were an hour or two later than it was, I should have continued to demand my men from this perfidious Yankee. I should have tried him with threats—have made some sort of a stand, at all events, and taken my chance of what was to follow. But if I was to regain my ship every instant was precious. It was darkening into night even as I paused for a few moments, half wild with anger and the hurry of my thoughts. My men were hidden; and my suspicions, indeed my conviction, assured me that I might shout for them till I was hoarse to no purpose. Then, again, the American vessel was now at every beat of the pulse widening the distance between her and the Ocean Ranger. It was certain that my first business must be to regain my own vessel while yet a little daylight lived, and leave the rest to Captain Hoste; and without further reflection, and without pausing to look if the American captain had followed me out of the cabin, I dropped into the mizzen channels and thence into the jolly-boat that was towing close under, and cast adrift the line that held the boat to the ship's side. The little fabric dropped astern tumbling and sputtering into the wide race of wake of the ship that drove away from me into the dimness of the rain-laden atmosphere in a large pale cloud, which darkened on a sudden in a heavier fall of wet that in a minute or two was hissing all about me.

I threw an oar over the boat's stern, and, getting her head round for my ship, fell to sculling her

with might and main.   There was now a little
more wind, and the rain drove with a sharper
slant, but the small ridges of the sea ran softly
with the boat, melting with scarce more than a light
summer play of froth on either hand of me, as I
stood erect sculling at my hardest.   The heavier
rush of rain had, however, by this time touched the
Ocean Ranger, and she now showed as vaguely
as a phantom down in the wet dusk.   I could
barely discern the dim spaces of her canvas, mere
dashes of faint pallor upon the gloom, with the
black streak of her hull coming and going as my
boat rose and sank upon the swell.

I had not been sculling more than three or four
minutes when I perceived that Captain Hoste had
gathered way upon his ship.   She was, in fact,
forging ahead fast and rounding away into the west
in pursuit of the American, leaving my boat in con-
sequence astern of her out upon her starboard quarter.   It was very evident that the boat was not to
be seen from the Ocean Ranger—that Captain
Hoste imagined me still on board the American, and
that, observing the Yankee to be sailing away, he
concluded it was about time to follow him—though
this was a pursuit I had little doubt Hoste would
speedily abandon, for it was not hard to guess that

the Ephraim Z. Jackson would outsail the Ocean Ranger by two feet to one.

The consternation that seized me was so excessive that my hands grasped the oar motionlessly, as though my arms had been withered. I could do no more than stand gaping over my shoulder at the receding ships. As to shouting—why, already my vessel had put a long mile and a half between her and my boat; and though I could not tell amid the haze of the rain and the shadow of the evening what canvas she was carrying, I might gather that Captain Hoste was pressing her, by the heel of her tall dim outline, and by the occasional glance of the froth of her wake in the thickness under her counter.

I threw my oar inboards and sat down to collect my mind and think. My consternation, as I have said, was almost paralyzing. The suddenness of the desperate and dreadful situation in which I found myself benumbed my faculties for a while. I was without food; I was without drink; I was also without mast, sail, or compass, in a little open boat in the heart of a wide surface of sea, the night at hand—a night of storm, as I might fear when I cast my eyes up at the wet, near, scowling face of the sky and then looked round at the fast-darkening

2

sea, narrowed to a small horizon by the gloomy walls of rain, in the western quarter of which the American had already vanished, while my own ship, as I stood straining my gaze at the pale blotch she made, slowly melted out like one's breath upon a looking-glass. Yet, heavy as my heart was with the horror of my position, I do not remember that I was then sensible of despair in any degree. When my wits in some measure returned, I thought to myself, rascal as the Yankee captain has proved himself, he surely will not be such a villain as to leave me to perish out here. He will know, by the Ocean Ranger pursuing him, that Captain Hoste has not seen my boat. Then he will shorten sail to enable the Ocean Ranger to approach, and hail Captain Hoste to tell him that I am adrift some-where astern; so that at any hour I may expect to see the loom of my ship close at hand in search of me, within earshot, with a dozen pairs of eyes on the lookout and a dozen pairs of ears straining for my first cry.

That my drift might be as inconsiderable as possible, I lashed the two oars of the boat together, made them fast to the painter, threw them over-board and rode to them. But when this was done it was dark, I may say pitch dark; the rain fell heavily and continuously, and the wind sang through it in a sort of shrill wailing such as I had never before taken notice of in the wind at sea, and this noise put a new and distinct horror into my situation because of my loneliness. The froth of the streaming ripples broke bare and ghastly, and the run of the waters against the boat's sides filled the atmosphere with notes as of drowning sobbing. The cold of the night was made piercing by the wet of it and the quarter whence the wind blew. I was soaked to the skin, and sat hugging my shuddering body, forever staring around into the blind obscurity, and forever seeing nothing more than the mocking and fleeting flash of the near run of froth.

The breeze held steady, but something of weight came into the heave of the little ridges, and from time to time the chop of the boat's bows as she chucked into a hollow, meeting the next bit of a sea before she had time to fairly rise to it; from time to time, I say, some handfuls of spray would come slinging out of the darkness forward into my face, but nothing more than that happened during those hours of midnight gloom. Though never knowing what the next ten minutes might bring forth, I had made up my mind that I was to be drowned, or if not drowned then that I was doomed to some dreadful ending of insanity which should be brought about by hunger, by thirst, by that awful form of mental anguish which is called despair, and that if I were spared to see the sun rise I should never see him set again.

But the night passed—the night passed, and I remember thanking God that it was an August night, which signified, comparatively speaking, short hours of darkness. It passed, and the breaking dawn found me crouching and hugging myself as I had been crouching and hugging myself during the black time that was now ending, staring in my loneliness, and with a heart that felt broken, over the low gunwale of the boat at the rim of the sea which slowly stole out all round me in a line of ink against the ashen slant of the sky. It had ceased to rain, but the morning broke sullen and gloomy; the heavens of the complexion they had worn when the night had darkened upon them; the wind no stronger than before, yet singing past my ears with a harsh salt shrillness that had something squall-like in the keen-edged tone of it each time the head of a swell threw me up to the full sweep.

I stood up, weak and trembling, and searched the ocean, but there was nothing to be seen. Again and again I explored the horizon with eyes rendered dim by my long vigil and by the smarting of the salt which lay in a white crust about the eyelids and in the hollows, but there was nothing more to behold than the gray ocean, freckled with foam, throbbing desolately in the cold gray light to its confines narrowed by the low seat from which I gazed.

I had now no hope whatever of being searched for and picked up by my own ship. I did not doubt that she had pursued the Yankee, who had outsailed her and been lost sight of by her in the darkness, and that Captain Hoste, understanding the villainous trick that had been played upon him, but assuming that I, as well as the two men, had been detained by the American, had long ago shifted his course and proceeded on his voyage. I looked at my watch, but I had forgotten to wind it overnight, and it had stopped. By and by I reckoned the hour to be between eight and nine. There was no sun to tell the time by. Not until then was I sensible of hunger and thirst. Now on a sudden I felt the need of eating and drinking, and the mere circumstance of there being nothing to eat and drink—and more particularly to *drink*—fired my imagination, which at once converted thirst into a consuming pain, and I put my lips to my wet sleeve and sucked; but the moisture was bitter, bitter with salt, and I flung myself down into the bottom of the boat with a cry to God that, if I was to perish, my agony might come quickly and end quickly.

I believe I lay in a sort of stupor for some hour or more; then noticing a slight brightening in the heavens directly overhead, as though due to the thinning of the body of vapor just there, I staggered on to my feet, and no sooner was my head above the boat's gunwale than I spied a vessel steering directly for me, as I was immediately able to perceive. How far distant she was I could not have said, but my sailor's eye instantly witnessed the course she was pursuing by the aspect of her canvas, that was of a brilliant whiteness, so that at first I imagined her to be the American in search of me, until, after viewing her for some time steadfastly, I perceived that she was a large topsail schooner, apparently a yacht, heeling from the wind, and sliding nimbly through the water, as one might tell by the rapidity with which the whole fabric of her enlarged.

The sight gave me back all my strength. I sprang into the bows, dragged the oars inboard, and to one of them attached my coat, which I went to

work to flourish, making the wet serge garment
rattle like the fly of a flag as I swept it round and
round high above my head. Within half an hour
she was close to me, with her square canvas aback
to deaden her way, the heads of a number of people
dotting the line of her rail—a shapely and graceful
vessel indeed, with a band of yellow metal along
her waterline, dully glowing over the white edge of
froth, as though some light of western sunshine
slept upon her, her canvas gleaming like satin, a
spark or two in her glossy length where her cabin
portholes were, and the brassy gleam of some gilt
effigy under her bowsprit, from which curved to
the masthead the lustrous pinions of her jibs and
staysail.

A red-headed man wearing a cap with a naval
peak stood abaft the main rigging in company with
others, and as the beautiful little vessel came softly
swaying and floating down over the heave of the
swell to my boat, he cried out, "Can you catch hold
of the end of a line?"

"Ay, ay," I answered, in a weak voice, lifting
my hand.

"Then look out!" he bawled.

A seaman grasping a coil of rope sprang on top
of the bulwarks and sent the fakes of the line spin-

ning to me. I caught the end with a trembling
grasp and took a turn round a thwart, but not till
then could I have imagined how weak I was, for
even as I held the rope my knees yielded and I
sank into the bottom of the boat in a posture of
supplication, half swooning. The next moment the
little fabric had swung in alongside the schooner;
I was grasped by some sailors and lifted on board.

"Let the boat go adrift, she's of no use to us,"
the red-headed man cried out.

Another standing near him exclaimed with a
strong foreign accent, but in good English, "Stop!
what name is written in her?"

Some one answered, "The Ocean Ranger, London."

"Let that be noted, and then let her go," said
the voice with the foreign accent.

In this brief while I stood, scarcely seeing
though I could hear, supported by the muscular
grip of a couple of the seamen who had dragged me
over the side.

"Bring a chair," exclaimed the red-headed man.

"No," cried the other with a foreign accent,
"let him be taken into the cabin and fed. Do not
you see that he perishes of hunger and of thirst
and of cold?"

On this I was gently compelled into motion by the two seamen, who conveyed me to an after hatch and thence down into a little interior that glittered with mirrors, and that was luminous and fragrant besides with flowers. I was still so much dazed as hardly to be fully conscious of what I was doing. Sudden joy is as confounding as sudden grief, and the delight of this deliverance from my horrible situation was as disastrous to my wits (weakened by the fearful night I had passed through) as had been the shock to them when I found myself adrift in the boat on the previous evening. The two seamen quitted the cabin, leaving me seated at the table, but their place was immediately taken by the red-headed man, by the gentleman with the foreign accent; and a minute later by a third person, a short, square, hook-nosed, black-browed, inky-bearded fellow. They viewed me for a while in silence; one of them then called "Tom," and a negro boy stepped through a door at the foremost end of the cabin.

"Bring brandy and water; also some cold meat and white biscuit. Bring the brandy first."

Who spoke I did not know. A tumbler of grog was placed in my hand, but my arm trembled so violently that I was unable to raise the glass to my lips. Some one thereupon grasped my wrist and enabled me to drink, which I did greedily, muttering, as I recollect, a broken " Thank God! thank you, gentlemen," as I put the glass quivering upon the table.

" How long have you been in this plight ? " inquired the red-headed man in a voice whose harshness and coarseness, half demented as I was, I remember noticing.

" Ask him no questions yet," exclaimed one of the others. " Let him have meat, dry clothes, and sleep, and he will rally. Ay! he will rally, for he has a lively look."

The effect of the brandy was magical. It clarified my sight as though some friendly hand had swept a cobweb from each eyeball. It filled my body with strong pulses, and enabled me to hold my head erect. But by this time the negro boy had reappeared with a plate of cold boiled beef and a dish of biscuit, and I fell to—eating with the animal-like rage of starvation. I devoured every scrap that was set before me, and then with a steady hand raised and drained a second glass of grog that had been mixed by the man with the foreign accent. And now I felt able to converse.

" Gentlemen," said I, making a staggering effort

to bow to them, " I thank you from the bottom of my heart for rescuing me from a horrible death. I thank you gentlemen for this bitterly-needed refreshment."

" You are soaked to the skin," said the man with the foreign accent. " You will tell us your story when you are dry and comfortable. Captain Dopping, you can lend this poor man some dry linen and clothes?"

" Ay!" responded the other, in his coarse determined voice. " Are ye able to stand?"

" I think so," I replied.

I rose, but observing that I faltered, he came round to where I was swaying, grasped me by the arm and led me to a little cabin alongside the door through which the negro boy had emerged. In this cabin were two shallow bunks or sleeping-shelves, one on top of the other. The room was lighted by a circular porthole, and by what is called a bull's-eye —a piece of thick glass let into the deck overhead. My companion rummaged a locker, and tossing a number of garments into the lower bunk, bade me take my pick and shift myself and then turn in, and, saying this in a harsh, fierce way, he withdrew.

I removed my wet clothes, and grateful beyond all expression was the comfort of warm dry apparel

to my skin, that for more than twelve hours had
been soaked with rain and steeped in brine. I then
stretched my length in the lower sleeping-shelf, and,
after putting up a prayer of gratitude for my deliverance, closed my eyes and in a few minutes fell
asleep.

I slept until about three o'clock in the afternoon. On waking I found the interior bright with
sunshine. I lay for a little, thinking and taking a
view of the cabin. My faculties, refreshed by
sleep, were sharp in me. I could remember clearly
and realize keenly. The disaster which had befallen me was a great professional blow. It had
deprived me of my ship, and robbed me of an ap-
pointment I had been forced to wait some tedious
months to obtain. With the ship had gone all my
clothes, all my effects, everything, in short, I possessed in the wide world, saving a few pounds
which I had left in a bank at home. The Ocean
Ranger was bound on a voyage that would keep her
away from England for two years and a half, perhaps three years ; so that for, let me say, three
years all that I owned in the world, saving my few
pounds, would be as utterly lost to me as though it
had gone to the bottom.

While I thus lay musing, the door of the berth

opened, and the red-headed man—Captain Dopping
—entered. Having my eyes clear in my head now,
I immediately observed that he was a freckled, red-
haired, staring man, with big protruding moist blue
eyes and scarlet whiskers; all of his front teeth but
two or three were gone, and the gaps in his gums
gave his face, when he parted his lips, the grin of a
skull.

I got out of the bunk when he entered.

"How do you feel now?" said he, eying me in
a hard, deliberate, unwinking way.

"Refreshed and recovered," said I.

He ran his gaze over my figure to observe what
garments belonging to him I had arrayed myself in,
then said, "What is your name?"

"James Portlack."

"What are you?"

"What *was* I, you must ask," said I, with a
melancholy shake of the head. "Second mate of
the bark Ocean Ranger," and I told him briefly
of the abominable trick which the Yankee captain
had played off on Captain Hoste, and which had
resulted in leaving me adrift in the desperate and
dying condition I had been rescued from.

"A cute dodge, truly," said he, without any exhibition of astonishment or dislike, nay, with a hint

in his air of having found something to relish in
the American's device. "It is what a Welshman
would call 'clebber.' This is a yarn to tickle Don
Christoval."

"Who is Don Christoval?" said I.

"He is Don Christoval del Padron."

"The owner of this schooner?"

He gave a hard smile, but returned no answer.

"What is the name of this vessel?" I asked.

"La Casandra."

"Where are you from?"

"Cadiz."

"To what port?" said I, with anxiety.

He gave another hard smile, and then, eying me
all over afresh, exclaimed, "Come along on deck.
Don Christoval and Don Lazarillo will be wanting
to see you, now you're awake."

I asked him to lend me a cap, not knowing
what had become of mine, and followed him
through the small brilliant cabin into which I had
been conducted by the two seamen. I had a quick
eye, and took note of many things in a moment or
two. The cabin was peculiarly furnished, that is,
for a sea-going interior. It gleamed with hanging
mirrors; the sides were embellished with pictures,
such as might hang upon the walls of a room

ashore; there were little sofas and arm-chairs, of a
kind you might see in a drawing-room, but not in
the cabin of a vessel, whether a pleasure-craft or
not. In short, it was evident that a portion of the
furniture of a house had been employed for fitting
out this interior. But where the vessel herself
showed, I mean the ceiling or upper deck, the sides,
the planks left visible by the carpet—*there* all was
plain and even rough, by which signs I might know
that La Casandra was not a yacht, despite the shining of the mirrors and the gilt of the picture-
frames, the rich carpet under foot, the crimson velvet sofas and chairs.

I followed Captain Dopping up the narrow
companion-steps, and gained the deck. The rain
was gone, the gloomy sky had rolled away down
the western sea-line, and the afternoon sun shone
gloriously in a sky of blue piebald with stately sailing masses of swollen cream-colored vapor, which
studded the blue surface of the sea with island-like
spaces of violet shadow. A pleasant breeze was
blowing, and it was warm with the sunshine. The
schooner was under all the canvas it was possible to
spread upon her, and how fast she was sailing I
might know by the white line of her wake. I had
no eyes at the instant for anything but the horizon,

the whole girdle of which I rapidly scanned with some wild silly notion in me of catching a sight of the cloths of the Ocean Ranger, that in searching for me might have been navigated some leagues to the north.

CHAPTER II.

THE two foreigners, as I might suppose them to be—the two gentlemen who had talked to me and viewed me in the cabin before I went to the captain's berth—these men were pacing the sand-colored planks of the quarter-deck arm in arm, cigars in their mouths, as I emerged ; but, on seeing me, they came to a halt. One was a truly noble-looking fellow, rising a full inch taller than six feet, and of a magnificently proportioned shape. This was the man who had addressed me in good English, but with a foreign accent. He was, besides, an exceedingly handsome person, his complexion very dark, his eyes of the dead blackness of the Indian's, but soft and glowing ; he wore a large heavy mustache, black as ink, and curling to his ears ; his teeth were strong, large, and of an ivory whiteness. Plain sailor-man as I was, used to the commonplace char-

3

acter and countenance of the mariner, I was without any art in the deciphering of the mind by gazing at the lineaments of the human face. To me
this person offered himself as a noble, handsome
man, of imposing presence, of a beauty even stately;
but when I think of him now in the light of that
larger knowledge of human nature which years
have taught me, when I recall his face, I say, I am
conscious of having missed something in the expression of it which must have helped me to a tol-
erably accurate perception of the *real* character of
this schooner's errand, when the "motive" of her
voyage was explained to me.

His companion was a short man, a true Spaniard
in his looks; his large hooked nose, his searching,
restless, brilliant black eyes, his mustaches and
short black beard might well have qualified him to
sit for a picture of Cervantes, according to such
prints of that great author as I have seen. They
were both well dressed—too well dressed, indeed.
They wore overcoats richly furred, velvet coats beneath, splendid waistcoats, and so forth. The fingers of the shorter man sparkled with precious
stones. There was a stout gold chain round his
neck, and a costly brooch in his cravat. They both
fastened a penetrating gaze upon me for some mo-

ments, and exchanged a few sentences in Spanish before addressing me.

"The gentleman's name is Portlack—Mr. Portlack, Don Christoval," said Captain Dopping: "he was second mate of a bark named the Ocean Ranger. He was hocussed, as the Pikeys (gypsies) say, by an American captain. He'll tell you the story, sir."

"How do you feel?" said Don Christoval.

"Perfectly recovered, I thank you," said I.

"I am glad. We were not too soon. I believe that another twenty-four hours of your desperate situation must have killed you," said this tall Don, delivering his words slowly, and looking very stately, and speaking in English so correctly that I wondered at his foreign accent.

"Vot ees secon' mate?" inquired the shorter man, pronouncing the words with difficulty.

"Why, you might call it second lieutenant, Don Lazarillo," replied Captain Dopping.

"It is a position of trust; it is a position of distinction on board ship?" exclaimed Don Christoval.

"Oh yes," said Captain Dopping.

"Do you know navigation?" asked the tall Don.

"I hold a master's certificate," I replied, smiling.

"Explain," said Don Lazarillo sharply, as though his mind were under some constant strain of unhealthy anxiety.

"I do not speak a word of Spanish," said I, turning to Captain Dopping.

"No need for it," said he, in his harsh accents. "A master's certificate, Don Christoval, enables the holder of it to take charge of a ship, and in order to take charge of a ship a man is supposed to know everything that concerns the profession of the sea."

"Explain," cried Don Lazarillo with impatience.

His tall companion translated; on which the other, nodding vehemently, stroked his mustaches while he again surveyed me from head to foot, letting his eyes, full of fire, settle with the most searching look that can be imagined upon my face. I caught Don Christoval exchanging a glance with Captain Dopping. There was a brief pause while the tall Don lighted his cigar. He then said, with a smile:

"You have lost your ship, sir?"

"I have, I am sorry to say."

"What will you do, sir?"

"It is for you to dispose of me. I should be

glad to make myself useful to you until you transfer me or land me."

" But then—but then ? "

" Then I must endeavor to obtain another berth," said I.

" Explain," cried Don Lazarillo.

Don Christoval spoke to him in Spanish.

" You are a gentleman by birth ? " said the tall Don.

" My father was a clergyman," I answered.

" Yes, sir, that is very good. Your speech tells me you are genteel. To speak English well you must be genteel. Education will enable you to speak English grammatically, but it will not help you to pronounce it properly. For example, a man vulgarly born, who is educated too, will omit his h's, and he will neglect his g's. He will say nothin', and he will say 'ouse instead of house. Yes, I know it —I know it," said he, smiling. " Well, you shall tell me now all about your adventure."

This I did. He occasionally stopped me while he interpreted to his companion, who listened to him with eager attention, while he would also strain his ears with his eyes sternly fixed upon my face when I spoke. When I had made an end, Don Christoval drew Captain Dopping to him by a backward

motion of his head, and, after addressing him in low
tones, he took Don Lazarillo's arm, and the pair of
them fell to patrolling the deck.

"We shall sling a hammock for you under the
main hatch," said Captain Dopping, walking up
to me. "Sorry we can't accommodate you aft.
There's scarce room for a rat in my corner, let alone
two men."

"Any part of the schooner will serve to sling a
hammock in for me," said I.

"You will take your meals with me in the cabin,"
said he. "I eat when the two gentlemen have done."

"Where does your mate live?" said I.

"I have no mate," he answered. "We were in
a hurry, and could not find a man."

He eyed me somewhat oddly as he spoke, as
though to mark the effect of his words.

"But is there no one to help you to keep a look-
out?"

"Ay! a seaman," he answered, carelessly. "But
now that you're aboard we will be able to relieve
him from that duty."

"Whatever you put me to," said I, "you will
find me as willing at it as gratitude can make a
man."

He roughly nodded, and asked me what part of

England I came from. I answered that I was born near Guildford.

"I hail from Deal," said he. "Do you know Deal?"

"Well," I answered; and spoke of some people whom I had visited there; gave him the names of the streets, and of a number of boatmen I had conversed with during my stay at the salt and shingly place. This softened him. It was marvelous to observe how the magic of memory, the tenderness of recollected association humanized the coarse, harsh, bold, and staring looks of this scarlet-haired man.

"But," said I, "you have not yet told me where this schooner is bound to."

"You will hear all about it," he answered, with his usual air returning to him.

I was not a little astonished by this answer. Had the schooner sailed on some piratic expedition? Was there some colossal undertaking of smuggling in contemplation? But though piracy, to be sure, still flourished, it was hardly to be thought of in relation with those northern seas toward which the schooner was heading; while as for smuggling, if the four seamen whom I counted at work about the vessel's deck comprised—with the fifth man, who was at her helm—the whole of the crew, there was nothing in any theory of a contraband adventure to solve the problem submitted by Captain Dopping's reticence.

He left me abruptly, and walked forward and addressed one of the men, apparently speaking of the job the fellow was upon. I listened for that note of bullying, for that tone of habitual brutal temper, which I should have expected to hear in him when he accosted the seamen, and was surprised to find that he spoke as a comrade rather than as a captain; with something even of careless familiarity in his manner as he addressed the man.

I had now an opportunity for the first time since I came on deck to inspect the schooner. It was easy to see that she had never been built as a yacht; her appearance, indeed, suggested that in her day she had been employed as a slaver. She was old, but very powerfully constructed, and seemingly still as fine a sea-boat as was at that time to be encountered on the ocean. Her bulwarks were high and immensely thick; the fore-part of her had a rise, or "spring" as it is called, which gave a look of domination and defiance to her round bows which at the forefoot narrowed into a stem of knife-like sharpness. She was very loftily rigged and expanded an

enormous breadth of mainsail. I had never before
seen so long a gaff, and the boom when amidships
forked far out over the stern. Her decks were very
clean but grayish with brine and years of hard
usage. I noticed that she carried a small boat hanging in davits on the starboard side, and a large boat
abaft the little caboose or kitchen that stood like a
sentry-box forward. This boat, indeed, resembled a
man-of-war's cutter—such a long and heavy fabric
as one would certainly not think of looking for on
board a craft of the size of La Casandra. It was
my sailor's eye that carried my mind to this detail.
No man but a sailor, and perhaps a suspicious sailor
as I then was, standing as I did upon the deck of a
vessel whose destination was still a secret to me,
would have noticed that boat.

The five of a crew were all of them Englishmen,
strong, hearty fellows. I inspected them curiously,
but could find nothing in them that did not suggest
the plain, average, honest merchant sailor. They
were well clothed for men of their class, habited in
the jackets, round hats and wide trousers of the
Jacks of my period, and I took notice that though
their captain stood near them they worked as though
without sense of his presence, occasionally calling
a remark one to another, and laughing, but not nois-

ily, as if what discipline there was on board the schooner existed largely in the crew's choice of behavior. These and other points I remarked, but nothing that I saw helped me to any sort of conclusion as to the destination of the little ship or the motive of the cruise. All that I could collect was that here was a schooner bearing a Spanish name and owned or hired by one or both of those Spaniards, who continued to pace the quarter-deck arm-in-arm, but manned, so far as I could see, by a company of five Englishmen and a negro lad, and commanded by an English skipper.

I walked a little way forward, the better to observe the vessel's rig at the fore, and on my approaching the galley, a fellow put his head out of it—making a sixth man now visible. He kept his head out to stare at me. Many ugly men have I met in my time, but never so hideous a creature as that. His nationality I could not imagine, though it was not long before I learned that he was a Spaniard. His coal-black hair fell in a shower of greasy snake-like ringlets upon his back and shoulders. One eye was whitened by a cataract or some large pearly blotch, and the other seemed to me to possess as malevolent an expression as could possibly deform a pupil unnaturally large, and still further disfigured

by a very net-work of blood-red lines. His nose
appeared to have been leveled flat with his face at
the bridge by a blow, leaving the lower portion of
it standing straight out in the shape of the thick
end of a small broken carrot. His lips of leather,
his complexion of chocolate, his three or four yellow fangs, his mat of close cropped whiskers, coarse
as horse-hair, his apparel of blue shirt open at the
neck and revealing a little gilt or gold crucifix, a
pair of tarry leather trousers, carpet slippers, and the
remains of an old Scotch cap that lay rather than
sat upon his hair ; all these points combined in pro-
ducing one of the most extraordinary figures that
had ever crossed my path—a path, I may say, that
in my time had carried me into many wild scenes,
and to the contemplation of many strange surprising
sights.

While this prodigy of ugliness and I were staring at each other, the captain came across the deck
to me.

"What do you think of this schooner?" he
said.

"She is a very good schooner. She is old—perhaps thirty years old. I believe she has carried
slaves in her time."

"I *know* it," he replied, with a strong nod, to

which his furiously red hair seemed to impart a character of hot temper.

"I have seen," said I, "handsomer men than yonder beauty who is staring at me from the galley door."

"Ay. He is good enough to shut up in a box and to carry about as a show. He is cook and steward. His name is Juan de Mariana. He cooks well, and is or has been a domestic in Don Lazarillo's establishment."

"How many go to your crew?" said I, questioning him with an air of indifference now that I found he was disposed to be communicative.

"Eight."

"The number includes you and the cook and the nigger lad?"

He nodded, and looked at me suddenly, as though about to deliver something on the top of his mind, then checked himself, and pulling out his watch, exclaimed: " I understand you are willing to serve as mate of this vessel."

"I am willing to do anything. Do not I owe my life to you all?"

"Well," said he, "that may be settled now. It is Don Christoval's wish. As to pay, him and me will go into that matter with you by and by."

I opened my eyes at the sound of the word *pay*, but made no remark. It was a grateful sound, as you will suppose, to a man who had as good as lost everything save what he stood up in, and who, when he got ashore, might find it very hard to obtain another berth. The two Spanish gentlemen had left the deck. Captain Dopping said: "Step aft with me," and we walked as far as the cabin skylight, where facing about the captain called out, "Trapp, South, Butler, Scott, lay aft, my lads. I have a word to say to you." He then turned to the fellow who stood at the helm and exclaimed, "Tubb, you'll be listening."

The seamen quitted their several employments and came to the quarter-deck. The Spanish cook stepped out of the galley to hearken, and a moment later the ebony face of the negro showed in the square of the forecastle hatch. The sailors looked as though they pretty well guessed what was coming.

"Lads," said Captain Dopping, placing his hand upon my arm, "this here is Mr. James Portlack. He was second mate of the bark, Ocean Ranger, a ship I know."

"And I know her, too," said one of the men.

"Mr. Portlack," continued Captain Dopping,

"holds a master's certificate, which is more than I do, and he tops me by that. But I'm your captain, and your captain I remain. Mr. Portlack consents to act as the mate of the Casandra. Is this agreeable to you, lads?"

"Ay, ay; agreeable enough," was the general answer.

"Well, then, Butler, you're displaced, d'ye see? No call for you to relieve me any longer."

"And a good job too," said the man, a heavy, sturdy, powerfully built fellow with small, honest, glittering blue eyes, and immense bushy whiskers; "there was nothin' said about my taking charge of the deck in the agreement."

"Well, you're out of it," exclaimed Captain Dopping, "and the ship's company's stronger by a hand, which is as it should be. D'ye hear me, cook?"

"Yash, yash, I hear all right, capitan," answered the swarthy creature from the door of his galley, contorting his countenance into the aspect of a horrid face beheld by one in a high fever, in his struggle to articulate in English.

"That'll do, my lads," said the captain.

The men leisurely rounded and went forward again. There was nothing unusual in this proceed-

ing. It was customary, it may still be customary at
sea, to invite the decision of the crew before elect-
ing a man to fill a vacant post as first or second
mate. All that I found singular lay in the behavior of the men. There was something in their bearing I find it impossible to convey—a suggestion of
resolution struggling with reluctance, or it might be
that they gave me the impression of fellows who
had entered upon an undertaking without wholly
understanding its nature or without fully believing
in the sincerity of its promoters. But be their
manner what it might, its effect upon me was to
greatly sharpen my curiosity as to the object of this
schooner's voyage from Cadiz to the north as she
was now heading.

I said to Captain Dopping, "I will take charge
at once if you wish to go below."

"Very well," said he, "I will relieve you at
four bells, and that will give you the first watch to
stand," by which he meant the watch from eight
o'clock till midnight.

"But I do not know your destination," said I.
"How is the schooner to be steered?"

"As she goes," said he with a significant nod,
angry with the scarlet flash of hair and whisker
which accompanied it.

"Right," said I, and fell to pacing the deck, while he disappeared down the companion-way.

Athirst as I was for information, I was determined that my curiosity should not be suspected. Be the errand of this little ship what it might, I was always my own master, able to say "No" to any proposals I should object to, though taking care to give due effect by willingness in all honest directions to the gratitude excited in me by my deliverance. I would find the fellow at the helm watching me with an expression on his weather-darkened face that was the same as saying he was willing to tell all he knew, but I took no notice of him, contenting myself with merely observing the vessel's course and seeing that she was kept to it. The voices of the two Spaniards and Captain Dopping rose through the little skylight, one of which lay open. They spoke in English, and occasionally I heard my name pronounced with now and then a sharp hissing "Explain" from Don Lazarillo, but I did not catch, nor did I endeavor to catch, any syllables of a kind to furnish me with a sense of their discourse.

All this afternoon the weather continued rich, glowing, summer-like. One seemed to taste the aromas of the land in the eastern gushing of the

blue and sparkling breeze.   The three white spires
of a tall ship glided like stars along the western
rim, but though we were in the great ocean high-
way nothing else showed during the remainder of
the hours of light.   Beyond a little feeling of stiff-
ness and of aching in my joints I was sensible of no
bad results of my night-long bitter and perilous
exposure in the jolly-boat of the Ocean Ranger.
I had, indeed, been too long seasoned by the sea to
suffer grievously from an experience of this sort.
Night after night off the black and howling Horn,
off the stormy headland of Agulhas, amid mount-
ainous seas, in frosty hurricanes whose biting breath
was sharpened yet by hills and islands of ice glancing dimly through the snow-thickened darkness, I
had kept the deck, I had helped to stow the canvas
aloft, I had toiled at the pumps, waist-high in
water, my hair crackling with ice, my hands without
feeling.   No! I was too seasoned to suffer severely
from the after-effects of exposure in an open boat
throughout an August night in the Portuguese
parallels.

At five o'clock, when I glanced through the
skylight, I spied the negro lad named Tom laying
the cloth in the little cabin.   Occasionally a whiff
of cooking, strong with onions or garlic, would

4

come blowing aft in some back-draught out of the
canvas. I judged that the crew were well fed by
observing one of them step out of the galley and
enter the forecastle, bearing a smoking round of
boiled beef and a quantity of potatoes in their
skins; then by seeing another follow him with
pots of coffee or tea, two or three loaves of bread,
and other articles of food which I could not
distinguish. Fare so substantial and bountiful
seemed to my fancy a very unusual entertainment
for a forecastle tea or "supper," as the last meal at
sea is commonly called.

I found myself watching everything that passed
before me with growing curiosity. The hideous
cook Mariana, followed by the negro boy bearing
dishes, came aft with the cabin dinner, and presently, when I peeped again through the skylight as I
trudged the deck in the pendulum walk of the look-
out at sea, I perceived the two Spaniards at table.
The several dyes of wines in decanters blended with
the brilliance of silver—or of what resembled
silver—and other decorative details of flowers and
fruit, and the square of the skylight framed a pictur-
esquely festal scene. It was possible to peep without being observed. The Spaniards talked inces-
santly; their speech rose in a melodious hum; for to

pronounce Spanish is, to my ear, to utter music.
But the majestic dialect was as Greek to me. Don
Lazarillo gesticulated with vehemence, and I never
glanced at the skylight without observing him in
the act of draining his glass. Don Christoval was
less demonstrative. He was slow and stately in
his movements, and when he flourished his arm or
clasped his hands, or leaned back in his chair to re-
volve the point of his mustache with long, large,
but most shapely fingers, he made one think of
some fine actor in an opera scene.

It was six o'clock by the time they had dined,
and at this hour the seamen taking the privilege of
the "dog watch"—but, indeed, it was all privilege
from morning to night in that schooner—were pacing the deck forward, four of them, every man
smoking his pipe—the fifth man being at the tiller.
I might now make sure that there went but five seamen to this ship's company. The ugly cook leaned
in the door of his galley puffing at a cigarette. The
sun was low, his light crimson; his fan-shaped wake
streamed in scarlet glory under him to the very
shadow of the schooner, and the little fabric, slightly
leaning from the soft and pleasant breeze, floated
through the rose-colored atmosphere, her sails of
the tincture of delicate cloth of gold, her bright

masts veined with fire, her shrouds as she gently rolled catching the western light until they burned out upon the eye as though of polished brass.

The two Spaniards arrived on deck, each with an immensely long cigar in his mouth. Don Christoval addressed me pleasantly in his excellent English. He asked me with an air of grand courtesy if I now felt perfectly well, inquired the speed of the schooner, my opinion of her, my experiences of the Bay of Biscay in this month of August, and inquired if I was acquainted with the coast of England, and especially with that part comprised between St. Bees Head and Morecambe Bay. His friend eagerly listened, keeping his fiery eyes fastened upon my face, and whenever I had occasion to say more than "yes" or "no," he would call upon Don Christoval to interpret.

Shortly after the tall Don had ceased his questions—and I found no expression in his handsome face and in the steady gaze of his glowing impassioned eyes to hint to me whether my replies satisfied him or not—Captain Dopping came up out of the cabin.

"Now, Mr. Portlack," said he, in his harsh, intemperate voice, yet intending nothing but civility, as I could judge, "get you to your supper, sir; eat hearty, and you can make as free with the liquor as your common sense thinks prudent."

I was hungry, having tasted no food since the meal of beef and biscuit which had been set before me when I was first brought on board; nevertheless I entered the cabin and took my place with some diffidence. I felt a sort of embarrassment in eating alone and helping myself—perhaps because of the shore-going appearance of the interior; it was like making free in a gentleman's dining-room, the host being absent. Tom, the nigger boy, waited upon me. He gave me a dish of excellent soup, and I fared sumptuously on spiced beef, some sort of dried fish that was excellent eating, potatoes, beans, fruit, and the like. The fruit was fresh enough to make me understand that the vessel was but recently from port. There were several kinds of wines in decanters upon the table; but two glasses of sherry sufficed me, though two such glasses of sherry I had never before drank. It might be that I was no judge, but to my palate the flavor of that amber-colored wine was exquisite.

The negro boy stood near waiting and watching me intently in the intervals of his business. Had the skylight been closed I should have put some questions to him, but the regular passage of the

shadows of the two Spaniards upon the glass of the
skylight as they walked the deck, warned me to be
very wary.   The change, not indeed from an open
boat, but from the decks and the cabin of the
Ocean Ranger to this interior, with its pictures,
mirrors, its handsomely equipped and most hospitable table, was great indeed, and as I looked
about me I found it difficult to realize the experience I was passing through.   I could now tell by the
weight of the fork and spoon which I handled that
the plate which glittered upon the white damask
cloth was solid silver.   There could be no doubt
whatever that the furniture of a drawing-room or of
a boudoir had gone to the equipment of this cabin.
Nothing seemed to fit, nothing had that air of
oceanic *fixity* which you look for in sea-going
decorations.   But a quality of tawdriness stole into
the general appearance through contrast of the gilt,
the looking glasses, the pictures, the velvet, with
the plain, worn sides of the vessel, the rude cabin
beams, and the gray and even grimy ceiling or
upper deck.   I asked the negro boy if he spoke
English.

" Yes, massa," said he, " I speak English, nuffin
else, tank de Lord."

" Were you shipped at Cadiz ? "

" Yes sah."

" I suppose they found you cruising about on the look-out for a job."

He showed his teeth and smiled broadly and blandly, in silence upturning his dusky eyes to the skylight. It was no business of mine to question him, but I thought it as likely as not that he had run from some American vessel, for it was hard to imagine that a lad who was undoubtedly a Yankee negro, and who I might fully believe was without a word of Spanish, would be idling in Cadiz.

I was about to go on deck when the boy said to me, " Do yah know where yaw've to sleep ? "

" In the 'tween decks I understood," said I.

" I'll show yah, massa, I'll show yah. Dis is de road to your bedroom, sah," and, somewhat to my surprise, he went to a little door at the foremost end of the cabin, opened it, and conducted me into a part of the schooner that was almost immediately under the main-hatch. The main-hatch was a very wide square, and the cover of it was formed of three pieces, one portion of which was lifted so that light and air penetrated ; the sun was still above the horizon, and I could see plainly. A hammock had been swung in a corner on the starboard side ; it was to be my bed, and there was no other

article of furniture; but then I was a sailor, very
well able to dispense with all conveniences, requiring
nothing but a bucket of fresh brine to supply the
absence of a wash-stand.   There was a quantity of
rope, some bolts of canvas, and other matters of that
kind stowed away down here.   The space, however,
was no more than a good sized cabin, owing to the
after bulkhead coming well forward and the forecastle bulkhead standing well aft.

Having taken a brief survey of my quarters,
heaving as I did so a melancholy sigh of regret over
the new sea-chest, the quantity of wearing apparel,
the nautical instruments, books and old home
memorials which the Ocean Ranger had sailed
away with, and which it was as likely as not I
should never hear of again, I re-entered the cabin
and mounted the short flight of companion steps.
Captain Dopping was walking with the two Spaniards.   I went a little way forward to leeward, and
leaned upon the rail, looking at the sea.   The
breeze was soft and pleasant, warm with the long
day of sunshine, and the schooner was sliding in
buoyant launchings over the round brows of the
wide heave of the swell which in the far dim east
swayed in folds of soft deep violet to the tender
magical coloring of the shadow of the coming night

that had paused in the heavens there. Four of the seamen were sitting in the schooner's head, watching with amused hairy countenances the face of the cook Mariana, who grotesquely gesticulated and contorted his form in his efforts to address them in English. On a sudden Captain Dopping crossed the deck, holding a handsome cigar case filled.

"Don Christoval wants to know if you smoke?" said he.

I took a cigar and lighted it at the stump which Captain Dopping was smoking, and perceiving that Don Christoval observed me, I raised my hat, and made him a low bow, which he returned with the majesty of a grandee. The captain resumed his place at the side of the two Spaniards, and I smoked my cigar alone, with wonder fast increasing upon me as I looked at the cigar, and then reflected upon the entertainment I was fresh from, and recollected how Captain Dopping had pronounced the word *pay*. What did it all mean? What mystery was signified, what proposals presently to come were indicated by this handsome, this hospitable reception of a distressed seaman—a mere second mate as I was or had been, rendered destitute by disaster—one of a crowd of obscure persons without pretensions of any kind or sort? Surely, had I been a

nobleman, a man in the highest degree important
and influential, this treatment could scarcely have
been more liberal and considerate.

I had nearly smoked out the exceedingly fine
cigar when Captain Dopping, in his rasping voice,
cried out to one of the men—I believe it was to the
man George South—to step aft and take charge of
the deck for a bit. I turned my head, and found
that the two Spaniards had gone below. Captain
Dopping beckoned to me, but the gesture was not
wanting in respect. He was but a Deal longshore
man, though superior to the ordinary run of those
fellows, and was impressed or, at all events, influenced by my holding a master's certificate and, let
me say it without vanity, for it is a thing to concern
me but little after all these years, by my speech,
manners, and appearance.

"You are wanted in the cabin," said he, and he
led the way below.

CHAPTER III.

DON CHRISTOVAL'S STORY.

Don Christoval and Don Lazarillo were seated at the table drinking coffee; the atmosphere was charged with the delicate aroma of the berry, blended with the perfume of choice Cuba tobacco. The hour was somewhere about seven. The sunset made the little space of heaven that showed through the skylight resemble a square of gilt. Spite, however, of there being some half-hour of twilight left, the two polished and gleaming silver cabin-lamps were burning.

"Pray sit," said Don Christoval. "I want to talk to you on an affair of business."

I took a chair. Captain Dopping seated himself opposite me. Don Lazarillo watched me with a fiery gaze of excitement and expectation.

"I will tell you plainly and at once, Mr. Port-lack," said Don Christoval, fastening his fine, burning, liquid eyes upon my face, "what the object of our expedition is. In a word, it is this: I am going to England to recover my wife, who has been feloniously stolen from me."

He paused to observe the effect of his words. I could only look blankly, for there was really nothing to be *thought* so far, and therefore nothing to be said.

"You will have suspected that our excursion was a singular one," said he smiling, with a note of sweetness threading his voice.

"I confess, sir," said I, "that I supposed this schooner to be on an errand which might be something a little out of the way."

"What does he say?" said Don Lazarillo in Spanish. Don Christoval patiently translated and then resumed, addressing me now with an air of melancholy and in tones curiously plaintive. "It is fit that my story should be told to you, because I shall desire your willing assistance. That story is well known to my friend, Captain Dopping, who did not engage the crew until he had made them acquainted with the object of this expedition. Captain Noble was in your Royal Navy, but he no longer serves. My mother, who I may tell you was an English woman, was distantly related to Captain

Noble on his mother's side. I met the captain and his daughter Ida in Paris, and," said he, with a graceful flourish of his hand, "I fell in love with the young lady. Captain Noble's wife is a woman of distinction. She is Lady Ida Noble, and her father is an earl. She did not favor my addresses, nay," said he, with his face darkening—and I observed that the countenance of Don Lazarillo, who was eying him steadfastly, darkened too in manifest sympathy with his friend's mood—"she was rude; she was repellent; she was insulting. She had high desires for her child, higher," he cried, smiting his breast, and rearing his form, and looking at his friend, "than Don Christoval del Padron." He gesticulated again. "Enough!—the lady, passionately adoring me, consented to elope. I had followed them to Madrid, and from Madrid my charming girl and I fled to London, where we were secretly married. The father tracked us. We were man and wife ere he discovered us. But, two days before we had arranged to leave England for Cuba, where I have an estate, I returned to the hotel where I had left my wife, and found her gone. I made inquiries, and gathered from the description given to me by the people of the hotel that Captain Noble and his son had called, had had an interview

with my wife, and that she had driven away with
them in the carriage in which they had arrived. I
easily guessed," he continued, speaking plaintively,
without the least temper, with an expression of
melancholy that wonderfully heightened the beauty
of his face, " that she had been made the victim of
some cruel stratagem. I knew she would write to
me when the chance was permitted her, and week
after week I lingered at the hotel, believing she
would address me there or return to me there.

"A month passed, and then I received a letter.
She informed me that her father and brother had
called and implored her to accompany them to her
mother, who lay in a dying state at a hotel in Bond
Street. She loved her mother, and her tender
heart was half broken by this afflicting intelligence.
Naturally, she made haste to accompany her father
and brother; but it was a base lie, Mr. Portlack,
an inhuman stratagem! They conveyed her, not to
her mother, but, valgamedios! to Captain Noble's
estate in Cumberland. There she has remained;
there she still is; but her deliverance is at hand, and
she awaits me."

"A regular mean and cruel business, don't you
think, Mr. Portlack?" cried Captain Dopping,
dragging at his scarlet whiskers.

"Does 'ee understand?" exclaimed Don Lazarillo.

"Perfectly," I answered. "It would be strange if I could not understand your pure English, sir," addressing Don Christoval.

"What we want to know is——" began Captain Dopping.

"Patience," interrupted Don Christoval, elevating his hand. "It is probable," he continued, turning to me, "that we may have to employ force. I hope not, but we are prepared," he added, with a flash in his eyes. "The lady is my wife: you will allow that I have a right to her?"

"Undoubtedly," said I.

"The marriage was in all senses lawful. I can produce the necessary documentary evidence. I can produce my dear one's letter in which she communicates to me the perfidious conduct of her father. You will own that I have a greater right to my wife than her father has to his daughter."

"You will own that?" rasped out Captain Dopping. "The law sets the husband first. He's afore all hands."

"That is so; that need not be reasoned," said I.

"Will you," said Don Christoval, "agree to assist me in obtaining possession of my wife?"

Don Lazarillo appeared to understand this question. He eyed me sternly and with inexpressible eagerness.

"Sir," said I, "you have saved my life and you have been very good to me. I should wish to be of service to you, though for no other reason than to prove my gratitude. But, sir, it would enable me to answer you, to learn the steps that are to be taken to recover the lady."

"That is easily done," exclaimed Don Christoval, with a sweep of his hand that made a single diamond upon his finger stream in an arc of white fire under the lamps. "Captain Noble's house is called Trafalgar Lodge. It is a house that stands amid grounds. It is situated on the coast of Cumberland, to the south of St. Bees Head. A walk to it from the shore occupies less than half an hour, so close is it to the sea. The cliffs are high, but there is a little bay that has a margin of sand which even at high water gives plenty of foothold for landing from a boat. Into this bay between the cliffs comes sloping a—I forget the name in English."

"A gap, Don Christoval?" said Captain Dopping.

"That is it—that is it. You walk up this gap into the country and then the house is not far off.

There is a little town about four miles distant inland—it is what you would call the nearest post-town to Trafalgar Lodge. It is a silent range of cliff—there are no guards of the coast. I have inquired, and there are no guards of the coast along that cliff. Well, when we arrive we keep what Captain Dopping calls a wide offing until the darkness of the night comes. We shall be guided by the weather: if it is fine we act, if it is stormy we keep at sea and wait. But suppose it fine. Good! We launch the boat. Myself, my friend here, Don Lazarillo de Tormes, Captain Dopping, and five seamen enter her and we land The rest is our affair. There must not be miscarriage; this voyage is costly." He glanced as he spoke at Don Lazarillo. " And we must go ashore in such force as to assure myself of getting possession of my wife, let Captain Noble and his son and his men servants and any gentlemen guests who may be sleeping in his house—let them, I say, oppose us as they will. But "—he held up his forefinger with a smile that made his teeth glance like light under his heavy black mustache—" what meantime is to become of this schooner? Do you see? The men we have we must take ashore, saving Mariana and Tom."

5

"The long and short of it is, Mr. Portlack," here broke in Captain Dopping, with a note of impatience hardening yet his harsh utterance, "there wasn't time to ship more hands in Cadiz. Don Christoval had received news that if he wanted to get possession of his lady he must bear a hand, for she stands to be carried abroad by her father, and that 'ud signify a constant shifting of places. We wanted more men, and Don Christoval would have no sailors but Englishmen. I scraped together the best I could collect in a hurry, but our company was too few by one or two for this here job. There's a house to be surrounded, d'ye see; there's a chance of one or more of us being hurt in the melhee that's likely as not to happen, and then again a man must be left in charge of the boat."

Don Christoval listened with patience, watching me; Don Lazarillo, in a fiery whisper, asked his friend to translate. This was done, and a short pause ensued.

"What you wish me to do," said I, "is to take charge of the schooner while you and the crew are ashore?"

"That is it," cried Don Christoval.

"With me you leave Mariana and the negro boy?"

" So."

" A slender ship's company if it should come on
to blow on a sudden," said I, smiling.

" We shall leave the vessel snug," said Captain
Dopping, " and we don't reckon upon being more
than three hours gone. Besides, we shall be guided
by the looks of the weather. It's still summer
time, ain't it ? "

" You see, Mr. Portlack," said Don Christoval,
leaning back in his chair and infusing a peculiar
note of sweetness into his voice, " you are a navigator and my friend Captain Dopping is a navigator.
It would be rash for both navigators to go ashore.
Suppose an accident should befall Captain Dopping
—how should we reach Cuba : nay, how should we
reach a near safe port ? There is no navigation
among us saving what you and he have."

" I understand, sir. I also gather that when you
have regained the lady you proceed forthwith to
the island of Cuba ? "

" To my estate there," he answered.

" You'll be able to see your way through this
job ? " exclaimed Captain Dopping. " The law's at
the back of us. A man has a right to his own.
There's no lawyer agoing to gainsay that, you know.
If you steal my watch and refuse to hand it over,

there's no law to hinder me from coaxing you into my view of the business with a loaded. pistol."

"Explain, in the name of the Virgin," hissed Don Lazarillo, in Spanish, for these words I could understand, and such was his excitement and impatience that the rings upon his trembling hands danced in flashes like rippling water under a light.

Don Christoval interpreted, on which the other bestowed several approving nods upon Captain Dopping

"But I have not yet spoken," said Don Christoval, "of any reward for your services. I here offer you fifty guineas, which shall be paid to you on our arrival in Cuba."

"Do you assent, Señor, do you assent?" whipped out Don Lazarillo, who now and again would catch the meaning of what was said.

The offer was a tempting one. It was made to a man rendered bankrupt by disaster. The money would go far to supply my loss; then again, my immediate business when I reached a port, no matter where it might be situated, must be to find a berth, and here was one prepared for me, easily and comfortably to be filled by me. Moreover, I was but a young man, and there were such elements of wild and startling romance in this Spaniard's proposal as could not fail to eloquently appeal to my love of adventure and to my delight in everything new and stirring. It was not for me to too curiously inquire into the sincerity of Don Christoval's story. Captain Dopping believed it; the five seamen believed it; and what was there for me to ground suspicion upon?

I paused but a minute and then said, "I accept, sir."

"Good!" cried Don Christoval, with enthusiasm.

He went to a locker, and took from it a small, richly-inlaid box or desk, which he placed upon the table; then on a sheet of gilt-edged paper, in the corner of which was stamped or embossed in colors a nosegay of flowers, with a legend in Latin upon a scroll beneath it, he wrote as follows:

> "*La Casandra, at Sea,*
> "*August 9, 1838.*

"*I, Don Christoval del Padron, hereby undertake to pay to Mr. James Portlack, acting as first mate of this schooner, the sum of fifty-two pounds ten shillings sterling on the vessel's arrival at Cuba.*"

He affixed his signature, and the document was further signed by Don Lazarillo and Captain Dopping as witnesses.

"This is the form of my agreement with Captain Dopping and with the sailors," said Don Christoval, handing me the paper. "I trust it satisfies you;" and he gave me one of his noble grandee bows.

"Oh, yes, sir, and I am obliged to you for it. I suppose the crew will be discharged on the vessel's arrival at Cuba?"

"Ay!" exclaimed Captain Dopping.

"I have but one more question to ask. Is your Cuban port fixed upon?"

"Matanzas will not be far off," replied Don Christoval.

Matanzas I knew to be near Havana; and at Havana, whose harbor in those days was populous with ships, I felt I should have no difficulty in obtaining a berth and so making my way home.

I rose, bowed, and went on deck.

The sun was gone; the night had fallen; it was hard upon eight o'clock. The wind had slightly freshened, and the schooner was slipping nimbly but quietly over the dark surface of the waters. There was a slip of young moon in the south-west, by which sign I might know that, if we made good progress, there would be moonlight for the wild midnight adventure we were embarked on. There was a growling murmur of sailors' voices forward in the gloom; aft, sliding up and down against the brilliant dust of stars over the stern, was the lonely shadow of the helmsman gripping the tiller; the seaman who had been commissioned to keep a lookout trudged in the gangway. My watch on deck would come round at eight o'clock, that is to say, in a few minutes. I leaned against the rail to think, but my reverie was almost immediately broken in upon by Captain Dopping. He approached me close, and peered to make sure of me, and said:

"Well, now you are one of us, what think ye of the job?"

" I have not yet had time to think," said I.

" It is good pay," said he, "and no risk to you either. You're on the right side of the door anyway. There's bound to be a scrimmage. The house is an old, strong building, there are gates to pass, and we must look to be fired upon."

"That you must expect," said I. "But you are numerous enough—seven powerful men, not counting the eighth, whom you leave to tend the boat. You will go ashore armed, of course?"

" Of course."

"You do not doubt that it is a genuine business?" said I.

"No, no," he answered in his file-like tones; "it's genuine enough. What d'ye suspect?"

"Why, do you see, an errand of this sort, Captain Dopping," said I, hushing my voice, "might signify anything else than the recovery of a Spanish gentleman's wife."

"So it might," he answered; "but in our case it don't happen to. You'll be satisfied when you see the lady brought aboard."

"Who is Don Lazarillo?" said I.

"A bosom-friend of Don Christoval's. I look to him more than to the other for my money. Plenty he has; ye may guess that by his hands."

"But my agreement is with Don Christoval."

"He'll pay ye—he'll pay ye."

"How did you meet him?"

"I heard that he was making inquiries for a master to take charge of this schooner. I was piloting a Spaniard to the Thames when she was run into, and they sent for me to Cadiz; and I had finished my business, and was thinking of getting home again, when this job fell in my way."

Pulling out his watch, he stepped so as to bring the dial plate into the sheen round about the skylight, then calling out that it was eight bells, and that the course of the vessel was the course to be steered, he vanished.

The Spaniards arrived on deck to smoke, and they walked up and down, constantly talking very earnestly in Spanish. But they never offered to accost me until they went below, at about half-past nine, when they both wished me good night, after Don Christoval had addressed a few words to me about the weather and the time we were likely to occupy in our run to the Cumberland coast. But though they went below, they did not go to bed. The negro boy placed fruit, wine, and biscuit upon the table, and the two Dons went to cards, each of them smoking a long cigar. There was something dream-like to me in the sight of them, along with the fancies begotten by the strange situation I now found myself in. It was like taking a peep into a camera obscura to glance through the skylight at the picture which it framed. Don Christoval looked a noble, handsome creature indeed, in the irradiation of the soft oil flames of the sparkling silver lamps. His smiles played like a light upon his face, so white were his teeth, so luminous the glow of his dark eyes at every festal sally of his own or his friend. Was his tale to be doubted ? Surely he was a sort of man to inspire a most romantic passion in a woman; and, given that passion, all that he had related was perfectly credible and consistent.

Likely as not, Don Lazarillo was finding the money for this adventure. Captain Dopping had said so, and, indeed, one had only to think of the schooner's equipment, and to peer down into that gleaming interior, to guess that the cost of this amazing quest must heavily tax even a very long purse. Don Christoval had talked of his estate in Cuba; he might be a poor man, nevertheless; his poverty, indeed, might have proved one of the objections which Captain Noble and his wife had found unconquerable, though their daughter had thought otherwise. It was quite conceivable then that Don Lazarillo, being an intimate friend of Don Christoval, should be helping him by his purse, his sympathy, and his association.

But speculations of this sort were not very profitable. I had myself to consider, and it reconciled me, I must own, to the adventure to reflect that the part I was expected to play in it was a passive one. The law of England in those times was not what it now is. Men were hanged for offenses which are now visited by short periods of imprisonment. If I was being betrayed into a felonious confederacy, I might hope to be safe in the plea of ignorance, and in the excuse of having taken no active share in what might happen. Another consideration : suppose I had declined Don Christoval's proposal, how should I have been served? I could not imagine they would speak a passing ship to transfer me to her. They were in a hurry, and not likely, therefore, to delay the run to the Cumberland coast by entering a port to set me ashore. So I must have remained on board in any case, and being on board, assuming the act they were intent on an illegal one, I should have been as much or as little incriminated as I now might be by agreeing to serve as mate in the vessel.

For eight days, dating from the morning of my rescue, nothing of sufficient interest happened to demand that this story should stand still while I tell it. We had extraordinarily fine weather; never once did the breeze head us so as to divert the schooner by as much as half a point from her course. Twice it blew fresh enough to single reef our canvas for us, but the breeze was a fair wind; it filled the sky with flying shapes of white vapor, but it left the sun shining brilliantly in the clear blue hollows between, and on these occasions it was that La Casandra showed her sailing qualities; for during thirteen hours the log regularly returned her speed as at something over twelve and a half knots in the hour. She heaped the foam to her stem head, and flashed it in dazzling clouds from her bows, and the race of it spread away astern like the boiling yeast from the beat of the wheels of a paddle-steamer, with a sparkling hill of sea steadfast on either quarter, and over those fixed curves of brine the froth swept like lace endlessly unrolling.

I punctually took sights every day with Captain Dopping, and every day, therefore, knew the exact position of the schooner at noon. The point of coast we were making for lay a few miles to the south of St. Bees Head. I reckoned that we should be off it by about the 18th. As the days passed, indeed I may say as the hours passed, the Spaniards grew visibly more anxious. Their laughter was infrequent, their conversation earnest and often agitated, as I might reasonably suppose by the tones of their voices and by their demeanor; they came and went restlessly, one or the other of them often appearing on deck in the night watches, and they never sat long at table.

But their behavior was perfectly consistent, entirely natural, such as was to have been expected in men who had embarked on a wild romantic advent-

ure, heavily laden with possibilities of tragedy.
They had very little to say to me, nor were their
conversations with Captain Dopping as frequent as
before. They kept much together, walking arm in
arm, Don Christoval grave to austerity, Don Lazarillo energetic in gesticulation, often pausing to
withdraw his arm to smite his hands with vicious
emphasis of what he might be saying, and all their
talk, as I might imagine, was wholly about the probable issue of this attempt to obtain possession of
Señora del Padron.

I had many opportunities of speaking to the
seamen. I warily questioned them, and one or two
appeared convinced that the object of this expedition was as had been represented to them, while the
others owned that though they did not doubt Don
Christoval's story, it might not be exactly as he had
put it, either.

"But what does it signify?" a man named
Scott said to me in one middle-watch while I conversed with him as he stood at the helm. "If
when we gets ashore and we find out that the job's
different from what we've been made to believe it,
why, sir, here stands one," said he, thumping his
breast, "who'll find it easy enough to say 'No' if
he means 'No.' There's no blazing furriner in all

Europe, let alone a Spaniard, as is good enough for
an Englishman to get into a mess for. This here
Don says he wants his wife, and I suppose his
money's as good as any other man's. Well, we're
willing for to help him to get his wife, and as his
tarms are handsome we're quite agreeable to a bit
of a shindy when it comes to our marching up to
the house and asking that the gent's lawful wife
should be restored to him. But if it ain't that,"
said he, squirting a mouthful of tobacco juice over
the stern, "if it's to be something that we haven't
agreed for, some job as might end in a prison hulk
and a free passage to Australia, here stands one,"
he repeated, striking himself afresh, "as 'll find it
easy to say 'No,' if so be as 'No' is the meaning
that's in his mind."

This, as I collected from the short chats I held
with others of the men, fairly represented the senti-
ments of the schooner's forecastle on the subject of
our expedition.

We had hauled on a course a trifle more west-
erly than was necessary to secure ourselves a wide
offing, and then, somewhere about one o'clock on
the afternoon of the 18th, we shifted our helm and
headed the yacht east-north-east. All hands were
on deck on the look-out for the land, the pale blue

loom of which might now at any moment be visible on the sea-line. The wind was about south, the day clear, hot and tranquil; there was a terrace of swollen white vapor down in the west, with a look of thunder in the knitted texture of the brows of the stuff, but the mercury in the barometer stood high, and I could find nothing to disquiet me in the appearance of the English heavens, tessellated here and there with spaces of high-poised, delicate cloud that gleamed with divers hues like the pearly inside of a mussel-shell.

Lunch had been served on deck to the two Spaniards. I noticed a change in Don Christoval; his face had hardened, there was an air of sneering temper in his rare smile that reduced it to little more than a mirthless grin, and often a vindictive look in his eyes as he would stand staring ahead at the sea, swaying his noble figure to the heave of the deck. His manner, indeed, suggested itself as that of one who seeks for courage in temper, for resolution in the evocation of hot thoughts. Don Lazarillo was pale as though oppressed with nausea. He constantly raised his hat to press a large silk pocket-handkerchief to his brow. When I glanced at him I'd wonder whether, when the hour came, he would be among those who entered the boat.

A small brig, a collier, with dingy ill-fitting canvas, her yards braced sharp up, passed under our stern near enough to hail us, but we took no notice of the old fellow who stood flourishing his hand upon the rail; whereupon to mark his disgust he flung his tall, weather-worn hat down on to the deck, and shook his fist at us with a shout whose meaning did not catch my ear, though a laugh arose among the men forward. The cook Mariana showed himself very agitated. He was constantly in and out of his galley, running into the schooner's head to stare, then darting back afresh to his pots and pans, one moment popping his hideous face out from the door to starboard, then thrusting it through the door to port, making one think of those little toy monsters which spring out of a box when you free the lid.

At four o'clock the land was in sight. The giant St. Bees Head dimly shaded the sea-line in the north-east, and thence the shore stretched in a blue film to the south, dying out in the azure atmosphere. Don Christoval leaned over the rail viewing the land with a face darkened by an immovable frown, the scowling air of which gave a malevolent expression to his eyes. He stood rooted—motionless—his hand with a paper cigar between his fingers, half raised to his mouth, as though the whole form of him had been withered by a blast of lightning.

"How close do you mean to sail, Capitan?" cried Don Lazarillo, sputtering out his words brokenly, with such an accent as could not possibly be imitated in print. "We shall be seen!" he exclaimed, with his face working with agitation.

"No fear of our being seen at this distance, Don Lazarillo," answered Captain Dopping. "A four mile offing is all we want till nightfall, and that there land is three times that distance off."

Don Lazarillo asked Don Christoval to explain, but the tall Spaniard continued to stand as though in a trance.

An hour passed, all remained quiet aboard the schooner. The light wind fanned the clipper keel of the craft forward, and by the expiration of the hour the land was hard, firm, and defined, but with no feature of spur, chasm, or ravine visible as yet to the naked eye. Sail was shortened to the extent of the topsail being furled, a jib hauled down, and the gaff-topsail taken in.

"Best see, while there's plenty of time and daylight," said Captain Dopping to me, "that the boat's all ready for launching," and then addressing

6

Don Christoval, he exclaimed, "Shall we get the arms-chest up, sir, and the weapons served out? It may come on a dark night," he added, sending a look at the terrace of cloud in the west, "and it won't do to mess about with lanterns."

"Do whatever you think proper," whipped out Don Christoval in accents fierce with excitement, though by his stern, hard, and frowning face it would have been impossible to guess his agitation.

I superintended the clearing away of the boat, and saw that everything was in readiness for launching her. This was to be done smack fashion—that is to say, by running her through the gangway over the side. Meanwhile a couple of seamen brought up a large square black box. Captain Dopping opened it, and disclosed a number of cutlasses and heavy pistols of the old-fashioned type. He called to the seamen and handed them each a pistol and a cutlass. I watched their faces as they received them. They all of them handled the weapons as objects strange to their grasp, with awkward grins running over their countenances as they poised the firearms in their brawny fists or drew the cutlasses to examine their blades.

"I hope," said the man Andrew Trapp, "that

it ain't going to come to our using these here tools?"

"The lady's to be got possession of," said Captain Dopping, "without spilling blood if it can be managed; but to be got, anyhow."

"That's right enough," said the sailor named South, "but all the same," said he, leveling the pistol he held, "if so be as I am to fire this here consarn, I choose that it shouldn't be at a fellow countryman."

"Mind dat pistole," cried Don Lazarillo, recoiling a step.

"I take it," said the seaman named William Scott, gazing earnestly at the cutlass in his hand, "that these weapons are meant more to what they calls overawe the people in the house we're to surround than to be used agin 'em."

"We may have to exert force," said Don Christoval, who stood near listening; "if our lives are threatened we must be in a position to protect ourselves. Is not this as you would wish, men?"

There was a general murmur of assent.

"I claim my right—no more!" the tall Spaniard cried, with an impassioned gesture of his arm; "you will help me to assert my right? I trust no blood may be shed—if blood is shed it will not be our fault."

"That puts it correctly, I *think*, lads?" exclaimed Captain Dopping, in his harshest voice and with his most thrusting manner.

The sailors holding their weapons went forward. Were they to be trusted at a pinch, I wondered? Assuredly they were not to be trusted in any sense if the business they were about to enter upon should prove in the smallest degree different from the object of the expedition as represented by Don Christoval.

We continued to stand in for the land under small canvas, which, however, there was no further occasion to reduce, for as the sun sank the wind fined down, and at seven o'clock the breeze had scarce weight enough to hold our sails steady. The sun was astern of us, and his light streamed full upon the coast, which glowed red as copper in that atmosphere upon the dark blue of the water brimming to its base and against the violet of the eastern sky. When the little collier brig which had spoken us sank her topmost cloths past the rim of the ocean, the sea line ran flawless from St. Bees Head right away round to the point where the land melted out. It was hard to credit that we were in

home waters, so deserted was that wide surface.
The schooner might, indeed, have been softly rippling through the heart of some Pacific solitude.

With the aid of a powerful telescope, handed
to me by Don Christoval, I could distinctly make
out the bay where the boat was to go ashore, and
the dark scar of gap or ravine vanishing in the land
beyond. I had never before been off this coast,
and ran the glass along the line of it, but I could
see no houses, no habitation of any sort; it was
sheer rugged cliff, whose character of forbidding
desolation was not to be softened by the rich and
beautiful light that at this hour clothed it. I asked
Captain Dopping if he was acquainted with this
coast, and he answered that many years before he
had made a trip to Whitehaven, which lay round
the corner to the north of St. Bees Head. That
was all he knew of the Cumberland shore. Occasionally Don Lazarillo would descend into the cabin,
and twice on glancing through the skylight I
detected him in the act of pouring out with a
trembling hand a full bumper of sherry, which he
seemed to swallow furtively, but looking round instead of *up*, possibly forgetting the deck window
through which I peeped. These draughts began to
tell upon him; his face grew flushed, his fiery eyes

moist, and his gait changed into a defiant strut when he moved restlessly about his friend, talking with extraordinary vehemence and a frequent snap of his fingers. Don Christoval, on the other hand, exhibited a new phase of mood. There was less of gloom in his face, more of animation. He smoked his cigar collectedly, with now and again a smile, and sometimes a laugh at what his flushed-faced, restless, gesticulating companion said. I took it that the English blood in his veins kept his nerves steady without obliging him to imitate Don Lazarillo's quest after courage in the contents of a decanter of wine.

I remember the sunset that night as one of sullen and thunderous magnificence. The luminary, like a huge red rayless target, sank into the coast of cloud over the stern, setting fire to the round and tufted shoulders of the long, compacted mass, but darkening the base of it into an ugly livid hue. Long beams of light, like the spokes of some titanic wheel of flame, projected in burning lines till their red and storm-colored extremities were over our mastheads; and as they slowly fainted, the coast ahead of us darkened, the blue of the sky beyond it deepened into liquid dusk with a single rose-colored star faintly trembling in the heavens almost directly above the bay that was our destination, as though it were some freshly kindled beacon to advise us how to head through the approaching gloom.

We continued slowly to stand in. The stem of the schooner scarcely broke the quiet water, and I reckoned that unless more wind came we should not have arrived at a point where we were to come to a stand much before midnight. The moon rose somewhere about half-past eight. She soared in a swollen mass of crimson out of the inky dye of the land, but swiftly changed into clear silver. Astern of us there was a constant play of red lightning, with an occasional moan of thunder slipping over the dark soft folds of the small swell. The two Spaniards, Captain Dopping, and myself stood near the helm.

"The moon," said Don Christoval, "shines full upon our white canvas, and reveals us."

"But first of all," said Captain Dopping, "who's keeping a look-out yonder? And next, supposing there to be eyes on the watch, who's to guess our business? Wouldn't any man who may already have twigged us through a glass reckon us a gentleman's pleasure-yacht from the Isle of Man, say, sauntering inward in view of this quiet night with a chance of a calm atop of it? But if you like,

Don Christoval—though it's not what I should rec-
ommend—we'll stand in a mile or two farther, then
douse every stitch, and ride to a short scope. The
soundings 'll be about twenty fathom."

"That will look suspicious," said Don Christoval. "I do not like the idea. I do not advocate
anchoring. See the time that will be lost in heaving up the anchor."

"What ees it dat Capitan Dopping say?" inquired Don Lazarillo.

His friend explained; on which Don Lazarillo
cried out shrilly, "No, no, no," and addressed Don
Christoval in Spanish with incredible vehemence of
delivery and gesticulation, his friend meanwhile uttering the single word "Si!" in a soothing note
over and over again.

"But if this breeze takes off, Captain Dopping," said I, when I could get an opportunity to
speak, "you'll either have to bring up or take your
chance of the schooner drifting far enough to make
the pull from the shore to her a long one."

Captain Dopping stared round the sea, whist-
ling.

"How far off is the land?" said Don Christoval.

"Call it six mile," answered the captain.

"It would be too far to row," said Don Christoval. "We must creep farther in."

"At what hour, sir," I asked, "do you wish to land?"

"It must be past midnight," answered the Spaniard, "when the house is hushed, and when, should firearms be used, there will be no one awake in the country around to hear the reports."

"And how long is the job going to take us, I wonder?" said Captain Dopping, cutting off a piece of black tobacco with a big clasp knife, whose blade glittered in the moonlight, and burying the morsel in his cheek.

"An hour—easily in an hour," answered Don Christoval, speaking rapidly and breathing swiftly. "Mark now how I piece out the time: three quarters of an hour to row ashore, half an hour to march to the house, that makes an hour and a quarter; an hour in executing our errand, that makes two hours and a quarter; and then another hour and a quarter to regain the schooner, that makes three hours and a half in all. Call the time four o'clock when we sail away, by five we shall be out of sight of land."

CHAPTER IV.

A MIDNIGHT THEFT.

It fell a stark calm at ten o'clock, and then I believed that there could be nothing for it but to bring up—that is, to let go the anchor; but half an hour later the moonlight upon the water—for by this time the moon had floated southward — was tarnished by a little air of wind from the south and west; it breathed, wet with dew, like a sigh into the schooner's canvas, then softly freshened into a small summer night-wind. The mass of clouds in the west had vanished; all was clear heaven from the sea line there to the looming shadow of the land over our bow; the moon rode high, small and piercingly clear; the canvas shone like ice in the light; stars of diamond-like brilliance sparkled in the moisture along the rail; and every man's shadow lay at his feet upon the pearl-colored planks, as though drawn in Indian ink there. The hush of expectation lay upon the little vessel as she crept along with a noise of rippling water refreshingly rising from alongside. Captain Dopping held his watch to the moon.

"Wants but twenty minutes to midnight," said he; "we're close enough in. Down helm," and he began to sing out orders in a voice whose harshness sounded startlingly upon the ear amid the exquisite serenity of that moonlit night.

The men ran about, still further reducing sail. So clear was the night, it was possible even at a distance to read the expressions upon their faces. There was no Preventive Force or Coastguard Service then as now. The English coast was indeed watched at certain parts of it where smuggling was notoriously carried on, and the people who kept a look-out were styled blockaders; but the northern reaches, more particularly where the coast was rugged and high, and where the facility for "running" goods, as it was called, was small, were unsentineled. The smuggler needed the accommodating creek, the comfortably shoaling foreshore, secret hiding places, and, above all, a handy local machinery for the prompt distribution of his commodities. All this was to be found in the English Channel, more particularly in that stretch of it which lies between the North and South Forelands; but it was not to be met with up here, on this lonely iron-bound Cumberland coast. In our time, even in these times, when smuggling is a decaying, an almost extinct business, the pallid apparition of such a schooner as La Casandra hovering doubtfully at midnight off any point of the English shore would infallibly in a very short time win the regard and invite the visit of a boat full of brawny coastguards, armed, as our men were about to arm themselves, with pistols and with cutlasses.

"Get the boat launched, my lads," called out Captain Dopping.

The gangway was unshipped, the muscular fists of the seamen gripped her gunwales, and she was run with a note of thunder overboard, stern foremost, smiting the water a blow that lashed it white, then lying quietly in the shadow of the schooner. The two Spaniards descended into the cabin, Don Lazarillo talking noisily as he trod upon his companion's heels. I stood looking on while Captain Dopping and the seamen girded the cutlasses to their hips and thrust pistols into their pockets or breasts.

"You will keep a bright look-out for us, Mr. Portlack," said the captain. "Hold the schooner as stationary as possible. There's nothing going to hurt her to-night," said he, with a look round, "and there'll be no tide to speak of for another two hours. You will then wear and keep her with her head to the nor'ard."

"Ay, ay, sir. But suppose, while you're ashore, a boat should come off and speak us?"

"Not likely, not likely," he rasped out.

"But suppose it, Captain Dopping. I accept no responsibility. What am I to say, and what am I to do?"

"Don't Don Christoval and his friend mean to come?" he answered, walking to the skylight and looking down.

Either he could not invent any instructions, or he considered a visit from a shore boat as a thing too improbable to merit consideration.

The two Spaniards came on deck. I had never supposed that Don Lazarillo would have had courage to enter the boat until I observed that he had armed himself with a long saber, the extremity of whose steel scabbard was visible at the skirts of the Spanish cloak he had drawn over his shoulders. Don Christoval was similarly swathed, but how armed I am unable to say, as no weapon was to be seen upon him.

"All's ready for the start, gentlemen," exclaimed Captain Dopping.

"Right!" exclaimed Don Christoval in a firm, deep voice, "let the men enter the boat."

The sailors dropped into her one by one, and sat silent and grim and dark in the gloom of the schooner's side, waiting.

"Where is Mariana?" cried Don Christoval.

The ugly cook's voice answered from somewhere forward, and he approached. Don Christoval addressed him in Spanish impressively, and as it seemed to my ear menacingly, emphasizing his words with frequent gestures. Mariana responded humbly with many shakes of the head, as though in deprecation of what had been said to him. Don Christoval then turned to me and extended his hand.

"Mr. Portlack, I rely upon your vigilance and seamanship. We hope not to be long absent."

He relinquished my hand, I raised my cap, and without another word, he, Don Lazarillo and Captain Dopping stepped over the side.

"Shove off," the captain exclaimed, and in a few moments the boat was gliding shoreward to the noise of the rhythmic grind of her five long oars betwixt the thole-pins, with eddies of dim phosphorescence under each lifted blade.

I watched her until her small shape, blending with the shadow thrown by the high land upon the water, was lost to sight, and then stepped aft to the helm, at which stood the negro boy Tom, who had been ordered to the tiller by me when the steersman had relinquished it to enter the boat. I mechanically eyed the illuminated disk of compass card, while my thoughts accompanied the armed expedition that was making for the shore. I figured the arrival of the boat at the margin of white sand that curved with the bay; in fancy I saw the people get out of her, leaving one behind to watch, and marching in a little dark company up the gap, a faint noise of the clank of side-arms attending them. In imagination I marked them cautiously approach the house —but what sort of house was it? Walls I had heard it had, and gates, and these must be forced or scaled. But what of Madame del Padron, the Ida of Don Christoval's heart, if not of his hearth? Was she lying awake yonder, expecting her husband? Impossible! for no date could certainly have been fixed for the arrival of the schooner off the coast. But of course she would be awaiting him with im-passioned anxiety at all hours of the night—nights that were gone, and to-night that was going: and he would have told her that he meant to regain her with the aid of an armed crew of seamen. Yet, though forewarned, should a struggle happen, she would listen with terror to the sound of fire-arms, to explosions, which might signify the death of her husband, or the fall of one or more of her own people, only a little less dear to her than her husband. What was her age? Was she dark or fair? Beautiful I could not but imagine the heroine, or, rather, the object, of such an adventure as this must be.

Then from musings of this sort my mind rambled into reflections of the odd and perilous fortune that had brought me into this business. How had fared the two sailors whom the murderous rogue of a Yankee skipper had pilfered from me? Into what-parallels had the Ocean Ranger penetrated by this time, and what man of her crew had been selected to fill my place? I looked at the negro boy, whose eyes in the moonlight resembled a brace of new silver coins set in a block of indigo.

"What's your other name?" said I.

"Tom, sah."

"Ay, but what besides Tom?"

"Tom ober and ober again, massa, as often as yah like."

"How old are you?"

He grinned widely as he answered, "Nebber was told, sah."

"Are you a Roman Catholic?" said I, talking sheerly for the want of something to do, and imagining he might have been chosen by Don Christoval because of his religion.

He shook his head, still broadly grinning, but meaning that he did not understand.

"Have you any religion?"

"Yes, sah."

"What is it?"

"I believe dat when I die I shall be seen no mo'."

"Where do you go when you die?"

"I know, sah," he answered, with a low throaty laugh.

"Where?" said I.

"Dis child," said he, touching his body, "goes dar," and he pointed down; "dat child," he continued, indicating his shadow that stretched sharply defined upon the planks, "goes up dar," and he pointed upward.

"Who taught you that?" said I.

"Is it true, massa?"

"Mind your helm," said I, "and I'll talk to you another time."

I went to the side and peered. The atmosphere in the south-west was brimful of moonshine, and the

7

sea line mingled with the sky in the delicate haze of sheen till you could not tell heaven from water. Nothing broke the stillness but the voice of the wind-brushed ripples, unless it were the chafe of a rope on high or the gull-like cry of the sheave of a block stirred by a sudden strain. The shadowy figure of Mariana, the cook, restlessly paced the deck forward. He seemed to be keeping a sharp lookout, as I was. A flock of wild fowl passed high overhead; their cries as they swept, invisible, over our trucks made a strange, solemn, plaintive noise in the midnight silence that was upon the sea. Sometimes I believed I could hear the small remote thunder of surf echoing out of the line of land which, now that the moon was shining upon it, stood in a long pale spectral range.

I was thirsty and stepped below for a tumbler of seltzer and claret. I took a cigar from a box which stood upon the table, dimmed the cabin lamps, and returned on deck. Expectation, the constant obligation of keeping a penetrating lookout, made the time heavy. The moon floated into the western quarter, and slowly the orb lost its brilliance and took its rusty hue of setting, though it was still high above the horizon. Nothing in the shape of a sail was visible the wide sea round; I was able to sink my sight to the confines of the water, but never could see the dimmest apparition of a ship.

Some time before three o'clock I wore the schooner, and waiting until she regained the point at which the boat had left her, I brought her head to the wind and held her so with her canvas trembling to the breeze. It was shortly after I had done this that my eye was taken by a faint redness ashore. The rim of the cliff turned black against the dim crimson light. It might have passed as the first of the lunar dawn—as though another moon were rising beyond the land to replace the orb that was sinking in the west. Mariana came out of the bows and called out to me with his incommunicable accent:

"Señor, do you see?" and he pointed to the light.

"Yes," said I, "that looks like a fire ashore. Whether the house has been fired by design or mischance, our people will have to bear a hand; for should there be any sort of country-side thereabouts it'll be swiftly up and wide awake and running and shouting to *that* signal."

He grunted, evidently without understanding a word of what I had said, and went forward again.

I had just glanced at the cabin clock and observed that it exactly wanted five minutes to four when my ears were caught by the sound of oars working in their pins. A moment later we were hailed in a voice thin with distance. I answered with a " Halloa! " at the top of my lungs. Presently the boat shaped itself out of the gloom that lay heavy upon the waters to the eastward. The gathering strength of the grinding noise was warrant that the men strained hard at their oars. The boat came shearing and hissing alongside as though her stem were of red-hot steel ; the oars were flung in and a boat-hook arrested the fabric's progress.

I stood at the side in the open space of the schooner's gangway. My eye was instantly caught by the figure of a woman supported in the arms of Don Christoval. One sees a thing quickly, and in the breathless pause between the arrival of the boat and what next happened I had time to note that the woman rested perfectly motionless as though dead, that her head was uncovered, and that her left arm lay like a stroke or dash of white paint in the gloom with a scintillation of gems in the dim gleam of some gold ornaments upon her wrist. Indeed, imperfect as my view was of her, I might yet know that she was in ball attire !

Three or four seamen came bounding out of the boat; the voice of Don Christoval exclaimed:

"Is that you, Mr. Portlack?"

"It is, sir."

"Captain Dopping," he cried, "has been shot dead. We were forced to leave him behind. The command of the schooner devolves upon you. This lady is in a heavy swoon, and must be lifted over the side. Let it be done instantly, pray; there is no time to lose."

I was greatly startled and shocked to hear of Captain Dopping having been shot dead and left behind, but the general agitation of the moment, the obligation of hurry, the wild impatience of the Spaniard, that hissed feverishly through his words, gave me no time to think of anything but what we had in hand. Don Christoval, muscular and big as he was, was unable, no doubt through exhaustion, to rise with the burden he supported. Don Lazarillo, addressing him in Spanish, sprang on board the schooner. I ordered a couple of seamen to assist Don Christoval, and the lady was lifted over the side and received by Don Lazarillo and Mariana, who straightway bore her below. I believed her to be dead. She never stirred, or uttered the least sound.

" Are all returned, saving the captain ? " I called out.

" All returned, sir," answered the gruff voice of one of the seamen.

" Anybody wounded ? "

" Nobody hurt, saving the captain, who was shot dead," responded the same voice.

Don Christoval, with a stagger in his gait, stepped out of the boat on to the deck, calling to me to give him my hand, lest he should fall backward.

" Be quick, and sail away, Mr. Portlack," said he, hoarsely. " A wing of the house caught fire, but through no fault of ours—no ! It was owing to the carelessness of some terrified servant within. Only one shot was fired ; it was meant for me, and slew Captain Dopping, who was at my side. That fire was a terrible signal—it may still be burning : I do not know ; all seemed in darkness when we gained the gap, but they rang a danger bell, a fearful summons that seemed to echo for miles and miles. Did you hear it here ? " he cried, almost gasping with the rapidity of his utterance.

" No, sir."

" Mounted messengers will have been flying from place to place long ago," he continued ; " they will send to Whitehaven, where, I heard our sailors say, there may be lying a Revenue cutter, or some more formidable ship of the State yet, to pursue us; therefore, for our lives' sake, Mr. Portlack, get the boat in and start at once."

He paused an instant to clasp his hands with an air of impassioned, theatrical appeal to me, then went below walking like a drunken man.

The bows of the boat were hastily hoisted into the gangway by means of a tackle called a burton. All hands of us then grasped the fabric, and dragged her bodily to her place on the deck. I could collect, by the motions of the men, that they were frightfully fatigued, but they worked with a will, as for their lives, indeed; well knowing—better knowing than I probably—what must be the fate of all hands of us if we were to be captured red-handed thus, with the house still on fire ashore for all we could tell—though I could now see no signs of the glow I had before observed—and with the dead body of the captain to fearfully testify to the audacious nature of this expedition.

Every stitch of sail the schooner carried was, cloth by cloth, expanded. Within ten minutes of the boat's return she was in her place on deck, the little topgallant-sail was being sheeted home, and La

Casandra, under full breasts of canvas, was sliding out into the gloom south and west. Clouds had collected in the west; and if the moon still hung over the sea, she could not show her face. Our course brought the weak damp wind a little forward of the beam. This was the schooner's best point of sailing, and she slided through it with a nimbleness that I hoped would put her out of sight of land before daybreak.

While the men, with weary motions, were coiling away the running gear which littered the deck, Mariana came up out of the cabin with a bottle of brandy. He told me that Don Christoval wished the sailors to drink. I said—

"Take it forward and serve it out; but see that no man gets more than a dram. If you muddle their brains, you will be putting us in the way of being hanged."

That he partly understood me I knew, by the energetic assent he howled out in his own tongue. I carefully swept the sea line, and then took a look through the cabin skylight. I had intended no more than a glance, but my gaze was arrested, as though fascinated by the spectacle it surveyed. Some one had turned up the lamps, and their flames burned brightly. Don Christoval sat at the table, supporting his head by resting his jaw upon his clinched fists. Don Lazarillo occupied a chair close to him; a tumbler, half full, was before him; he held an unlighted cigar, and his eyes were fixed upon the object at which his friend was staring.

This was no more nor less than the figure of a girl of about two-and-twenty, resting at full length upon a velvet couch. The remains of what might have been a wreath of flowers were in her hair. A portion of her hair, that was of a dark red, and that glowed like gold, as though it had been plentifully dusted with gilt powder, was detached, and lay in a long thick tress upon her shoulder. They had unclasped a rich opera cloak, and her attire was revealed. Her ball-dress of white satin, looped here and there with pink roses, was cut low, and exposed her throat and shoulders; but there were some ugly scratches on the flesh near her left shoulder. She wore very handsome jewelry: diamond earrings, a rope of pearls with a cross of diamonds that sparkled against the dark yellow of the tresses which had fallen. Her arms of faultless mold were bare to the short sleeves; her hands were gloved; I believed I could witness traces of blood upon the white kid; and her wrists were circled with bracelets.

But to describe all this is really to describe nothing: for how am I to convey to you the disorder of apparel that suggested a struggle which you must have thought deadly in its consequences, when you looked at her motionless shape, her closed eyes, her bloodless face, and the lifeless pose of her arms?

I stood gazing. Presently Don Christoval, extending a trembling hand, poured himself out half a tumbler of brandy—brandy I might suppose it was, by observing that he filled up the glass with water. He drained the tumbler, and suddenly looked up and saw me. He instantly rose and came on deck. He was without his hat. He seated himself on the corner of the skylight, where he commanded a view of the interior of the cabin, and called down some words in Spanish to Don Lazarillo, who nodded violently, but without removing his eyes from the girl.

"Does the schooner make good way?" said Don Christoval.

"Yes," I answered; "her speed is about five miles an hour."

"At dawn shall we be out of sight of the coast?"

"It will not be long before daybreak," said I,

"and at dawn the coast may be in sight of us, but I do not suppose we shall be in sight of it."

He stood up to look around the sea.

"It is sad," he exclaimed, "that Captain Dopping should have been shot."

"It is shocking," said I.

"You have sole control of the schooner now, Captain Portlack, for my captain I make you," said he. "And the money that I had agreed to pay to Captain Dopping shall be yours, in addition to the fifty guineas as arranged."

I gave him a bow and said, "Thank you." My eyes were fixed upon the motionless girl below; he was able to observe the direction of my gaze by the sheen of the lamplight, that rose like a haze through the glass and the lifted lid of the skylight.

"How cruel! how cruel!" said he, in a deep yet musical voice, that was not the less thrilling because of a certain indefinable flavor of theatricalism; "how cruel, that I should be obliged to claim what is mine by force, which I find barbarous when I look there," said he, pointing to the figure of his wife, "and when I recall Captain Dopping's cry as he fell lifeless at my side."

"Is your lady dead?" said I.

"No, no, I think not; indeed, I am sure not.

She is sunk in a trance or stupor. If she were bled, she would revive; but there is no man on board who has the skill to bleed her."

" She looks to have been very roughly handled."

" What you see," he cried, " is the work of her inhuman father and brother. Captain Noble, his son, and my wife had returned from a ball. We found the gate open, the carriage at the door : they had only just alighted, indeed, and the carriage was in the act of driving away; but the hall-door was closed. We knocked, and Captain Noble put his head out of a window and asked who was there. I told him that it was I, Don Christoval del Padron ; that I had arrived to take possession of my wife, whom he had forcibly divorced from me and was keeping a prisoner—that is, never leaving her out of his own sight or the sight of others of his family. He disappeared, and then returned to the window. I did not know he was armed. He shouted insultingly to us to be off. " Give me my wife ! " I cried. " I desire no struggle, no uproar. Give her to me, to whom she belongs, and we will withdraw peacefully." He fired, and Captain Dopping fell and died with a groan. On this we stormed the door ; we put a pistol to the keyhole and blew away the lock. Strangely enough, the door was not bolted.

No doubt, in the alarm our sudden appearance had caused, this had been overlooked, or possibly Captain Noble supposed that some one had shot the bolts. We entered; but what follows others may be better able to tell than I. All was confusion and cries. They had hidden my wife. We entered five rooms before we found her. This search was mine and Don Lazarillo's. The seamen guarded the door, and stood cutlass in hand over Captain Noble and his son. I found my wife locked in a room. When I turned the key and she beheld me she rushed to my arms with a cry of delight. I enveloped her in her opera cloak and conducted her downstairs, but on Captain Noble and his son beholding us they dashed themselves against the seamen, rushed upon us, and then it was that my wife suffered in her apparel and upon her neck, as you see. She fainted, she instantly became insensible. In the stupor that she now lies in we carried her to the boat. As we left the house I saw the red light of fire in a wing on the left, but it was not our doing; they can not charge that to me."

This extraordinary story he told in such broken-winded English as I have attempted to convey it in. While I listened, I had found it difficult to reconcile his statement that his wife had been imprisoned by her father with the circumstance of her having accompanied him and her brother to a ball. Then, again, while I listened, from time to time, looking at the figure of the girl as he spoke, I wondered, as I had before wondered again and again, in thinking over the object of this expedition, why, if the lady, as he had represented, had been all anxiety to rejoin her husband, should Don Christoval have considered it necessary to carry an armed force ashore with him? That she had not been a prisoner, in the sense of being confined to a room, or to a suite of rooms, was made manifest by the ball attire in which she lay as one dead upon the cabin sofa. Her liberty in a certain degree she must have enjoyed. Could she not, at some preconcerted signal, have stolen from the house secretly, and darkly joined her husband, and secretly and darkly sailed away with him, saving all this tremendous obligation of midnight landing and of armed seamen, with its tragic result of fire and a slain man, not to mention the condition of the wife, who, if not now actually dead, might be a corpse before the sun rose?

There might have been a pause of five or six seconds while I thus mused, during which I seemed to feel rather than see that his dark and burning eyes were scrutinizing me by aid of the cabin light that touched my face.

"The lady lies startlingly motionless, shockingly lifeless, Don Christoval," said I.

"But her pulse beats—her pulse beats."

"Shall you persist in sailing to Cuba, sir?"

"Certainly; we are now proceeding to Cuba," he exclaimed, and he half rose from the corner of the skylight as though with a mind to step to the compass.

"Cuba is a long way off," said I.

"What of that?" he cried, instantly, and with heat.

"Seeing the condition of that lady," said I, "I could not be sure but that you would wish to visit some near port to obtain medical help, and——"

"What?" he demanded, bending his head forward to observe me.

"Why!" said I, with embarrassment, because I was about to say something that might sound like impertinence in the ear of the Spaniard, "madame, your wife, Don Christoval, will not be expected by you to make a voyage to the island of Cuba in a ball-dress."

"I have provided for that," he exclaimed, haughtily. "I have minded my business, Captain

Portlack, and if you will mind yours all will be well." He immediately added in a softened voice, as though regretting any display of temper, " Yes, we must proceed to Cuba. If Cuba is erased from my programme, my arrangements will be rendered worthless. Besides, we have to-night done that which must oblige us, for every man's sake, to put as many leagues of water between ourselves and yonder country as this schooner can measure in a month. The Atlantic Ocean is not too wide for us after what has happened in the darkness this morning."

Just then the cook or steward Mariana came under the skylight and upturned his mask of a face. He addressed Don Christoval in Spanish. The other answered and was about quitting me, but stopped and said : " Let me see, Captain Portlack, I believe you sleep under the main hatch ? "

I said yes, that was so.

" Well, we shall not wish to disturb you. Don Lazarillo surrenders his cabin to my wife, and he takes that which Captain Dopping occupied. But any conveniences you may require, pray ask for, and you shall have them. I will take care that all the nautical instruments, the chronometer, the charts, and such furniture are conveyed to you."

He then went below. It was not proper that I should linger at the skylight as though I were a spy. I paced the deck, looking eastward for the first faint green of the dawn; yet my walk carried me so close to the skylight, and the length of deck I traversed was so short besides, that it was easy to see what was going on below without pausing or appearing to look. Still, what I saw was no more than this: that Don Christoval, his friend, and Mariana assembled at the side of the unconscious girl, where they appeared to hold a consultation; that when I passed the skylight in another turn, I observed them posturing themselves as though to lift her; and that when I once more passed the skylight in the third turn, the interior was empty—the lady had been conveyed to her berth.

Day broke a little later. The land showed dim against the dawn; and the distance we had made good during the hour of darkness had carried us, as I had foreseen, far out of eye-shot of any point of the range of cliffs. There was a small vessel standing to the north, abeam of us, and the sails of another, hull down, were shining upon the blue edge of the sea right ahead, as prismatically to the early piercing radiance of the now risen sun as a leaning shaft of crystal. I leveled a glass at her

8

and found that she was pursuing the course we were steering. There was nothing in sight where the shadow of the land was; but even if I had supposed we should be pursued, I was very sure we should not be caught. There was nothing, I might swear, flying the crimson cross, capable of holding her own with La Casandra. As to our being intercepted—life moved sluggishly in those days. Steamers there were indeed, but they were few, and none to be promptly prepared for sea to a swift summons. The electric telegraph did not exist. I can not say there were no railways; but I am certain that pursuit would have been long rendered hopeless before intelligence of what had taken place could be communicated to a port where the machinery necessary for an ocean chase was to be found and put in motion.

But, then, were we likely to be pursued? Who would be able to guess at our destination?

I paced the deck, depressed, anxious, full of misgiving. I heartily wished myself out of this business; yet I now stood so committed to it that I was at a loss to know how to act. The violent death of Captain Dopping was a shock to me. It sharply edged my realization of the significance of this midnight adventure. And now that the tragic business was ended there was something I found unintelligible in it, something which pleaded to my instincts, stirring and troubling them. Four sea-men sat to leeward of the little galley; they seemed to be dozing; their whiskered faces were bowed over their folded arms; a fifth man was at the tiller. I peered through the skylight and saw Don Lazarillo asleep in a chair. The man at the helm was William Scott; he had been there while Don Christoval talked to me, and I guessed that he had overheard every syllable of the Spaniard's narrative of the adventures of the party ashore. I stepped up to him and said:

"This has been a strange business."

"It has, sir."

"I am now in command here, as I suppose you know?"

"I didn't know, sir; but you're the one to take command, surely, now the captain's dead and gone."

"Yes, but it is a command I do not desire. I shall want a mate, some man to stand watch and watch with me. Did you hear Don Christoval tell me just now what happened ashore?"

"Yes, sir. His yarn was pretty near the truth; not quite, though."

"Where," said I, "was he mistaken?"

"The lady was insensible when him and the other Spanish gent brought her downstairs. It's true that her father and the young gentleman, her brother, bust from us when they see her being carried through the hall, but it is not true that she got them scratches upon her shoulder *then*. She was bleeding when the two Spaniards came along down the stairs with her. I took notice of them marks, and so did Tubb and Butler."

"Did her father, Captain Noble, say anything during the time you were guarding him—while you, or whoever else it was, stood watch over him ?"

"Ay, a deal more than my memory carries, sir. Yet it was nothing but calling names—nothing in the way of explaining matters. It was ' *The infernal villain !—The brutal wretch !—Who are these scoundrels?—Are you pirates, you ruffians ? —You speak English ; you are English ; will you help these two Spaniards, English as I reckon you to be, to kidnap an Englishwoman from her father's home in England ?* ' But if that had been all ! Butler, he flourished his cutlass and threatened to give the old gent a tap over the head if he didn't belay his jaw. Pirates we *wasn't !* We was ashore helping a gentleman to his rights. Captain Dop-

ping told us that the law was on our side, and
there's ne'er a pirate as can say *that* of his calling."

I continued to pace the deck a while musing on
this man's version of the adventure. The morning
opened wide and brilliant as the sun soared. Soon
after daybreak the breeze freshened, and the waters
were now streaming and arching into little heads of
foam as they ran with it. Mariana came out of the
cabin and was trudging forward when I called to
him:

"How is the lady?"

Instead of responding he shrugged his shoulders
till the lobes of his long yellow ears rested upon
them, proceeded to the galley and lighted the fire.
I went a little way forward and called to the seamen, who at daybreak had risen from their squatting
postures and now hung together talking in low
voices. They approached me. There were four of
them, Trapp, South, Butler, and Tubb; Scott still
grasped the tiller till he should be relieved at four
bells—that is to say, at six o'clock.

"Men," said I, " Don Christoval has asked me
to take charge of this schooner. You may have
heard him say so when he came aboard this morning."

"I heard him, sir," said Andrew Trapp.

"I shall want a mate," said I. "Butler, you filled that post under Captain Dopping. Will you take it afresh?"

"If I must, I must, sir," he answered gloomily. "No extra pay goes to the job, I suppose?"

"I can not tell you. Scott says that the lady's father behaved like a madman, and that you threatened him with your cutlass."

"That's true," answered Butler. "He called us pirates, and swore he'd have us hanged as pirates. I never was tarmed a pirate afore, and I lost my temper, but I did him no hurt."

"It's a job," exclaimed Tubb, "which I, for one, am sorry I ever meddled with. Yonder," cried he, pointing to the dim haze of land, "lies Captain Dopping, shot through the head. Had any man said it was a-going to come to *that*, I should have told the Don that *I* wasn't one of the sailors he was looking out for."

"That's a bad part of it," said I, "perhaps the worst part. But another very bad part is the condition of the lady. She looked to me, as she lay in the cabin, as if she had been very roughly handled."

The ugly cook put his head out of the galley

and stared at us. I called to him, in an angry voice, to bear a hand and get the men's breakfast, adding that they had been up all night and wanted the meal. " There's to be no loafing, no skulking, now, d'ye understand. We're too few as it is, and you're just one of those rusty pieces of old iron which want working up, Yankee fashion; so turn to, d'ye hear?" and I confirmed my meaning by a menacing inclination of the head. The ugly rogue vanished, but I could hear him muttering a number of Spanish oaths to himself.

"You were speaking of the lady, sir," said Butler.

"She looks," said I, "to have been rascally used. Her dress is vilely torn, as though in a struggle. Her shoulder is badly scratched, and why should she have fainted dead away, and why should she remain insensible for hours—insensible still, for all I know? For joy at seeing her husband?"

"She was carried down the stairs unconscious by the two Spaniards," said Tubb, "her clothes was tore then, and her flesh was scratched."

" Did the Spaniards mount the stairs alone?"

" Alone, sir," answered Butler. " Scott and me stood over the lady's father and his son; and South and Tubb guarded the door."

"Who remained in charge of the boat?"

"Me," said the man named Trapp.

"The name of the lady's father," said I, "is Captain Noble. Did he say nothing more to the point than to abuse you as pirates?"

"Nothing noticeable," answered Butler; "his wits seemed to be drove out of him by his rage."

"I heard him ask," said South, "how we, as English sailors, could help a scoundrel Spaniard to steal an English lady away from her father's house in England."

"Did he say *steal?*" said I.

"Force was the word he used—force an English-woman away. I didn't hear the word steal, George," said Butler.

"Is it a fine house?" said I.

"A regular gentleman's castle, sir," answered Butler. "We found the gates open; there was a carriage with a coachman and footman at the door; it was just a-driving off as we marched in."

"What became of that carriage?"

"I see the coachman pull up," answered South, "when he was near the gates. I kept my eye on the vehicle, for there were two men on the box of it. When the lock was blowed away, the coachman flogged his horses, and the whole concern disappeared. I expect they drove off to give the alarm, but where to, blowed if I know, for there looked to be no houses for miles around."

"What happened next?" said I.

But what the men now told me substantially corresponded with Don Christoval's story: saving that they were all agreed that the lady was insensible and in the disordered and torn condition in which she had been brought aboard when carried downstairs by the two Spaniards.

"Well," said I, "the schooner's decks must go without a scrubbing this morning. Hurry up that cook and get your breakfast. Butler, you'll relieve me at eight bells. I must find out how the lady is doing. If she's to die—and as she lay in the cabin she looked as if she were dying—Don Christoval will surely not want us to sail him to Cuba."

"But where else?" said Butler, nervously and suspiciously.

"To a French port, if you like—to any place that is near. I wish to get out of this ship."

"So do I," said Butler, looking at his mates, "but we want our money, Mr. Portlack, and we want to be landed in some part of the world where we aren't going to be nabbed for this 'ere job.

Let it be Cuba, if *you* please, sir. 'Tain't too far off—no, by a blooming long chalk, 'tain't too far off."

"Get your breakfast and relieve me at eight," said I, and I walked aft.

CHAPTER V.

MADAME.

Don Christoval remained out of sight below. I assumed that he was attending to his wife. His friend continued asleep in an arm-chair near the table under the skylight; his head was fallen back, his mouth was wide open, and his deep and powerful snore was audible at the distance of the helm. By and by the negro boy Tom rose through the companion hatch.

"Where is Don Christoval?" said I.

"In dah missus' cabin, sah," he answered.

"Has consciousness returned to her?"

He scratched his head and answered that he did not understand me.

"Have you heard the lady speaking—have you heard her voice?"

"Not speak, but sing, massa."

"Sing?" cried I, looking at him.

"Ay, massa, like dis:" he sang a few notes.

"Her song is all de same as a nuss-gal making him noisy pickaninny go for to sleep."

He went to the galley and presently returned with a tray full of breakfast things. Don Lazarillo was awakened by the negro lad laying the cloth for breakfast. I was at the skylight at the moment and my eye was upon the Spaniard. He started to his feet, delivered himself of a loud yawn, looked blankly around him with the stupid air of the newly awakened; the motions of his body were then arrested as though he had been paralyzed; he listened, intently gazing aft, continued to listen while you might count twenty, the expression of his face slowly changing from astonishment to terror. He then made a stride and disappeared out of the small range of view I commanded. I strained my ear but caught nothing unusual. He has heard the Señora del Padron singing, thought I.

The negro boy went again to the galley and once more returned with a second tray of dishes for the table. I was hungry and sleepy. Rest I might easily obtain by summoning Butler aft to keep a look-out, but I had no notion of turning in until I had breakfasted. I supposed that I should be expected to eat as heretofore, when Captain Dopping was alive in the vessel—that is to say, after the

Spaniards had left the table; and I was wondering
when Don Christoval meant to put in an appearance; at that moment he came on deck.

His face was colorless; I may say it was ghastly
with what I must term its pallor of swarthiness.
The peculiar hue seemed to enlarge his eyes.
He stood curling his mustaches a moment looking
around him, and then approached me with a shallow
and unquiet smile.

"All goes well with the schooner, I hope, Captain
Portlack?" said he.

"Yes, sir."

"How does the weather promise?"

"The day may keep fine, but I look for wind
presently."

"I am going to ask you," said he, with a harsher
Spanish or foreign intonation in his accent than I
had ever before noticed in his speech, "to be so
good, Señor Portlack," he raised his hat and held it
a little above his head, "to waive your custom of
taking your meals in the cabin," he put his hat on.
"I deplore the necessity. You will not regard it, if
you please, as a violation of the laws of hospitality—
laws by which we are eminently governed in our
country. Neither will you suppose that your estima-
ble society is not prized and your professional help

and attainments greatly valued by Don Lazarillo de Tormes and myself. But—" He abruptly ceased, giving me nothing more to interpret than a truly royal sweep of his arm.

"You wish me to eat in my own quarters, Don Christoval? I shall be happy to do so; but I presume I am to be waited upon?"

"Most undoubtedly," he burst out. "I entreat that you will speak every wish that may occur to you. Your apartment shall be furnished from the cabin: there shall be a table and all conveniences. Tom will see to you as he sees to us. I thank you for your ready assent;" and he gave me a stately bow, raising his hat again.

I returned his salute in the handsomest way I could manage, and inquired after his wife.

"Oh, she will do, she will do," he answered. "Patience! the shock was great and sudden; she expected me indeed, but there was nothing in expectation to soften the agitation excited by my sudden appearance. Add to this the inhuman behavior of her father and brother, their outrageous violent language, their grasping her," he continued, advancing his arms and opening and clinching his fingers as he acted the part, "in the hope of tearing her from me. But patience, Captain Portlack."

Then without another word he returned to the cabin.

At eight o'clock Butler came to the quarter-deck. I gave him the course, told him I should turn in for a couple of hours after breakfast, and bade him call me should the wind shift ahead, for we were in St. George's Channel, with the Irish coast on one side and the English coast on the other, and in case of our having to *ratch*, as it is called, La Casandra would need better piloting than Butler was equal to. I was about to quit him when he said :

" Beg pardon, Mr. Portlack, what might the Don have been a-saying just now ? " Then observing my change of expression, he quickly added, " The question's asked quite humbly, sir. The long and short of it is, we men don't feel comfortable. We want to make sartin that there's to be no putting in to any new port, and least of all to an English port."

I feigned not to understand him.

" So long as you receive the money that is agreed upon between you and Don Christoval it can not signify what port we put into."

" Oh, but it do, then ! " cried he, turning red in the face. " What ! Why, only consider ! " he con-

tinued, raising his voice for the edification of his
mates who stood listening forward. "Put into an
English port and see what 'ud happen! Put into
any civilized port and see what 'ud happen! I
know them Customs covies. What 'ud they find?
A lady in evening attire: us without any sort of
yarn capable of satisfying the suspicions we're
bound to raise. Why, all hands of us 'ud be detained for investigation, and then!"

"You may ease your mind," said I, coldly.
"Don Christoval was merely talking to me about
my breakfast," and going to the main hatch I
dropped through it into my quarters.

Here I found the furniture that had belonged to
Captain Dopping's cabin; there were also a little
table, a velvet arm-chair from the cabin, and a rug
such as would be stretched before a fire-place lying
upon the deck. My quarters, thus equipped, looked
hospitable enough. Indeed, it was to my taste to
live thus apart It rendered me independent; I
could do as I pleased, light my pipe, turn in or turn
out, eat and drink, and come and go with a bache-
lor-liberty that I should not have been able to enjoy
had I dwelt as Captain Dopping had in the cabin.
The one objection to my quarters lay in the gloom
of them. In fine weather there was plenty of light

to be obtained through the open hatch; but in stormy times the hatch must be closed, and then I should have to live by lamp-light.

A few minutes after I had descended, the door that communicated with the cabin opened, and the negro lad entered with my breakfast. He put the tray on the table, and stood as though expecting me to question him.

" Is the lady still singing?" said I.

" No, sah, ebery ting quiet now."

" That will do," said I, and he went on deck through the main hatch.

I made a hearty meal and smoked a pipe of tobacco—Captain Dopping had laid in a liberal stock of pipes and tobacco. I then pulled off my boots and coat, sprang into my hammock, and in five minutes was as sound asleep as the dead. Butler wakened me by putting his head into the hatch and shouting. I went on deck, and found my prediction to Don Christoval of a fine day disproved. The weather had thickened, the sky was a wide spread of shadow, under which a quantity of yellow, wing-like shapes of scud were flying with a velocity that might have made you suppose it was blowing a gale of wind. The wind was damp, but there was no rain. Blowing it was, but not yet

9

hard, and Butler had given no other orders than to roll up the topgallant-sail. The breeze was on the quarter, about north-north-west. Had we been working up against it we should have found it a strong wind; as it was, the schooner was swirling before it with every cloth set, saving the little sail I have mentioned. A strong swell chased her, and to each hurl of the regular, giant undulation the vessel flashed along, burying her bows in foam with the next launching swoop in a manner to remind you of the flight of a flying-fish from one glittering blue slope of brine to another.

The vessel that had been ahead of us at daybreak was now on the bow close to—a box-shaped concern with painted ports; she plunged heavily, and seemed to stagger again under her heights of canvas, like an old woman whose balance is threatened by the umbrella she holds up. Such a sputtering as she made I had never before beheld. All about her was white water as she washed through it; it was as though a water-spout were foaming under her. Yet she held her own stoutly; and, two hours after I had been on deck, she was still in sight in the haze astern.

I could make no use of Captain Dopping's sextant in such weather as this. Don Lazarillo was walking the deck alone, swathed to the heels in a cloak, and a large, flapping felt hat, drawn down to his eyebrows. He looked at me askew as I stepped his way to glance at the binnacle. Often had I met his fiery glance scanning me, but never so searchingly as now. He kept his eyes upon me as I stood at the compass watching the behavior of the little ship as she swept to the heads of the swell. When I moved forward, he advanced with a forced, deep grin which so contracted his visage that it looked no more than a mat of hair with a hooked nose thrust through it. He saluted me, and I bowed low, as was my custom with these gentlemen, and the following exchange of sentences took place, partly by signs, partly by shouts; but the substance of our meaning is all that I will venture to give. It would be impossible for the pen to convey his broken English, and as I have not a word of Spanish, I dare not attempt to write the sentences with which he intermingled his English.

"It is a very dark day."

"It is," I answered.

"It blows heavily."

"No, Don Lazarillo," said I.

"I thank the Virgin I am not seasick. Yet, the sight of those mountains," said he, pointing over the side with a yellow, jeweled hand, "makes me sensible that my stomach is of the most delicate."

"By this time you should have grown accustomed to the motion of a ship."

"Yes, it is so. Might not this dark day prove fatal to us?" Here he struck his fists together to denote a collision between vessels.

I shook my head and touched my eyes and pointed to the men forward, touching my eyes again that he might gather it was the custom of English sailors in thick weather to keep a look-out.

"How long to Cuba?" he asked.

I shrugged my shoulders. "Is Don Christoval still resolved to go to Cuba?" said I.

"Yes," he cried in Spanish, in the most passionate way that can be imagined, while an expression of dark suspicion entered his eyes. "You know the way to Cuba?"

"Oh yes," I answered smiling.

He nodded wildly as though he would say, "See that you carry us there, that's all!"

"How is madame?" said I, pointing to the skylight.

"Better—better," he replied, with a little scowl, and then giving me a bow he took a turn or two and went below.

The wind freshened gradually during the afternoon, and when I left the deck at four o'clock the schooner was under greatly reduced canvas, driving along at eleven or twelve miles an hour, her decks dark with damp, fountains of spray blowing ahead of her off the high archings of foam upturned by the irresistible thrust of her stem, a shrill, dreary noise of wind in her rigging, and the fellow at the helm and the figure on the look-out forward gleaming in oil-skins and sea-helmets.

All through the night it continued to blow, and it blew all through the three following days and nights. At long intervals one or the other of the Spaniards appeared on deck, but for no other purpose than to take a hurried look round. Some small theory of navigation, though utterly insufficient for practical purposes, they must have had; for, happening on one occasion during this boisterous time to look through the skylight glass, I perceived them bending over a chart. Don Christoval, with his forefinger upon it, seemed to trace a course, while he glanced up in the direction where there hung, screwed to the upper deck, what is known at sea as a "tell-tale compass," that is, a compass whose face is inverted, usually fixed over the captain's chair, so that, as he sits at table, he

may perceive at a glance whether the helmsman is
holding the vessel to her course.   I stood watching,
careless as to whether the Spaniards perceived me
or not.   The skylight was closed, and their voices
were inaudible.   Don Christoval seemed to explain;
Don Lazarillo measured : there was much nodding
and gesticulation, and they frequently looked from
the chart to the "tell-tale compass."   Presently
Don Christoval rolled up the chart, and the pair of
them withdrew out of reach of my sight.

I took notice that when Mariana was not employed at cooking in the galley, he was aft below
in the cabin.   I could not imagine what sort of
work the two Dons could find to put the ugly,
greasy rogue to in that part of the schooner.   I
now never entered the cabin, and could do no more
than conjecture what passed in it.   Regularly at
meal-times, if I happened to be on deck, I would
peep through the skylight window, expecting to
find madame at table ; and if it happened that I
was off duty when meals were served in the cabin, I
would tell Butler to cast a look through the glass
and report to me if he saw anything of the lady.
But my curiosity was punctually disappointed : the
lady remained invisible.

It happened that, on the evening of the third

day of this spell of dirty weather, I went below to
get some supper. It was seven o'clock, and the
evening dark as midnight with the driving thickness in the wind and the black surface of cloud
that was stretched across the sky. As I dropped
through the hatch, pulling the piece of cover over it
to keep the wet out of my quarters, I observed a
glare in the interior, which I very well knew could
not proceed from the lamp that swung under a
beam near my hammock. In fact that lamp was
unlighted. Looking past the bulkhead to which
the steps by which I descended were nailed, I found
that the door which communicated with the cabin
stood open. The wind, though abaft the beam,
gave a decided "list" or inclination to the rushing
fabric, and her rolls to windward, owing to the
swell being almost astern, were too inconsiderable to
cause the door to swing to.

The cabin was steeped in light; the lamps were
large for the interior, and burned brilliantly, and
their luster was duplicated and reduplicated by the
mirrors which hung against the side. Don Christoval lay at full length upon a sofa; his hand, droop-
ing to the floor, holding between its fingers an extinguished cigar, showed that he was asleep. Don
Lazarillo was either on deck or in his berth. The

dinner-cloth was upon the table, but cleared of its furniture, though on a large swing-tray between the lamps were one or two decanters of wine, a plate of fruit, biscuits, and the like. But that which instantly arrested my eye was the figure of Mariana seated on a chair at the after extremity of the cabin, where stood two berths. He bestrode his chair as a man strides a horse, bowing his hideous face to the back of it. His posture assured me that he was acting the part of sentinel. I stood viewing him. I could see no signs of the lady's presence, in the shape, I mean, of apparel, of any detail of female attire. I searched with my eyes swiftly, but narrowly, and encountered nothing to indicate the existence of a woman on board. What did I expect to see? I know not, unless it were something a lady might use, and leave on a chair or a table—a smelling-bottle, a glove; but this does not matter. I wished to discover if madame had left her berth, and I found no hint to inform me that she had done so.

But what signified the presence of that ugly, I may say that loathsome, sentry stationed at what I might make sure was the door of the berth she occupied? By the aid of the light flowing in from the cabin, I sought and found the materials for lighting my own lamp. I then quietly closed the bulkhead door.

A little later the hatch was lifted, and the negro boy descended with my supper—a repast consisting of cold meat, biscuit and fruit, and half a bottle of wine.

" Where is the cook ? " said I.

" In de cabin, massa."

" He appears to live in the cabin. What is he doing there now, d'ye know ? "

" Watching, sah."

" Watching what ? "

" Dah lady."

" Oh ! " said I, " watching the lady, hey ? Is she in her room ? "

" No, sah ; outside de door ob it Dey has to watch her," said he, showing his teeth.

" Why, do you know ? "

" I heered the tall Don say at breakfiss-time dat she was gone for mad."

After a pause I said, " When did you hear him say this ? "

" Yesterday morning, sah."

" To whom did he say it ? "

" To Mariana, massa. T'odder gentleman was sleeping."

I recollected that I had watched Don Lazarillo awaken from his sleep on the previous morning, and that I had observed the expression of terror his face had taken when, as I might *now* know, he learned for the first time, by hearing madame singing, that she had lost her mind.

"Why did you not, before this evening, tell me that the lady was gone for mad, as you call it?"

"Massa nebber asked dah question."

"Have you seen her?"

"No, sah, and I dun wan' to. Her laugh make my blood creep. It's wuss dan her singing, sah. Now and agin she laugh, but now she sings no mo'."

"How is she watched at night, do you know?"

He twisted his hand to indicate the turning of a key in its lock, by which I gathered that madame by night was locked up in her cabin.

"Is she watched?"

"Mariana him sometime sleep and sometime sit at her door. When him sleep, den Don Christoval keep watch. When Don Christoval sleep den t'odder gent keep watch. Dey makes tree watches ob it, sah."

I asked him how he knew this. He answered in his negro speech that he had found it out by looking and listening.

"But what are you to find out by listening?"
said I. "You don't understand Spanish, and those
three men among themselves talk in no other language."

"Mariana, him say to me in de galley, 'Tom,'
him say, 'you look to de sailors' pudden. De massa wan' me to keep watch in de cabin.' I say,
'Why you no sleep now in the fok'sle?' and he say
he hab business in de cabin."

Here the boy ceased; the poor fellow conveyed
his meaning with difficulty, yet I could see his
face working with the intelligence of an explana-
tion which lay in his brain, but which his tongue
wanted English to impart. That he knew the lady
was watched by the three Spaniards in the manner described by him — that is to say, in three
watches, by night at all events, if not by day—was
certain.

He left me. I ate my supper, lighted a pipe,
and sat musing. What had driven the lady mad?
One could not put it down to any ill-usage she had
met with aboard the schooner, because I might certainly know from the information of the negro boy
that she had awakened mad from the death-like
swoon or stupor she was plunged in when conveyed
from the boat into the cabin. Had her joy on find-

ing herself with her husband again—the husband
of her adoration—proved too much for her mind?
Had the sudden shock of his apparition—of the
apparition of Don Christoval and his six armed as-
sociates—been rendered too enormous for her poor
brains, through the fearful significance it gathered
from the slaying of Captain Dopping by her father,
and by her father's and brother's last rush and
struggle to wrest her from the hands of the two
Spaniards? But then the sailors were all agreed
that she was already insensible when this final rush
and struggle took place, that she was borne downstairs and carried out of the house bleeding and
unconscious as she was when I beheld her lying in
the cabin. A haunting suspicion grew darker,
stronger, harder within me.

.   .   .   .   .   .

I was again on deck at midnight; the weather
had somewhat moderated, but a strong sea was running, through which the schooner, under small canvas, crushed her way in thunder, whitening the
water around her till the black atmosphere of the
night about her decks was charged with the ghastly
twilight of the beaten and boiling foam. But before my watch expired the deep shadow on high
was broken up. A few stars sparkled, the seas ran

with less weight, and the diminished breeze enabled me to make sail upon the schooner.

The cabin skylight was closed, and owing to the moisture upon the glass it was impossible to see into the interior. Throughout the night the lamps were kept dimly burning, and ardently as I might peer, thirsty with curiosity, I never could distinguish the movement of a shadow to indicate that those who occupied the cabin were stirring in it.

At four o'clock I went to my hammock, and at half-past seven was on deck again. It was a fine clear morning; large white clouds were rolling over the dark blue sky, and the sea, swept by the fresh wind that hummed sweet and warm over the quarter, ran in delicate lines of foam, which writhed and twisted in confused splendor in the glorious wake of the sun; while westward, the surface of the deep resembled a spacious field lustrous with fantastic shapes of frost. Butler had heaped canvas on the schooner, and she was sliding nobly through the water. The men had washed the decks down, and hung about waiting for their breakfast. From time to time Mariana's head showed in the galley-door. So far, aboard of us, there had been no discipline to speak of. The men, indeed, acknowledged me as captain, and sprang to my commands; but outside such absolutely essential duties as that of making and shortening sail and washing down the decks of a morning, nothing was done. The fellows would hang about smoking and yarning, always ready indeed for a call, but nothing more. Nor, indeed, was it for me to keep them employed. I could not accept this adventure seriously—could not regard the command I had been asked to take as imposing any further obligation upon me than that of navigating the schooner to a part of the coast of Cuba adjacent to Matanzas, and again and again I would ask myself, Will it ever come to Cuba? Will it ever come to half-way to Cuba? There was an element of unreality in the voyage we were now supposed to be pursuing that submitted it as a mere holiday jaunt to my fancy—a purposeless cruise, rendering needless and aimless the customary shipboard routine of the sea.

While I stood looking along the deck, Don Christoval arrived. He was haggard and blanched, as though risen from a bed of sickness. The fire of his fine eyes was quenched, and his gaze was extraordinarily melancholy and spiritless. He saluted me gravely, but stood for some time as though lost in thought, meanwhile taking a slow view of the whole compass of the sea, as though in search of some object he expected to behold upon the horizon. I believed he would return to the cabin without addressing me; but I was mistaken.

"Good morning, Captain Portlack."

"Good morning, sir."

"The bad weather is passed, I hope. The schooner is sailing very fast. It rejoices me to reflect that every hour diminishes, by something, the tedious miles we have to traverse."

He paused, eying me steadfastly, with the air of a man soliciting sympathy. He then beckoned to me with one of his grand gestures and went a little way forward, out of the hearing of the fellow who stood at the tiller.

"Captain Portlack," said he, "I am in great grief."

"I am sorry to hear it," said I, looking at him.

"My poor wife is mad."

"Mad!" I echoed, in an accent of concern and astonishment, not choosing, by appearing aware of the fact, that he should suspect I had been spying upon him or making inquiries.

"Mad," he repeated, in a low, hoarse voice. "When she recovered from her swoon she did not know me. She began to sing, she laughed—Mother of God, a diabolic laugh ! She is now speechless, never lifting her eyes, never changing her countenance, and she sits thus:" he clasped his hands before him, bent his head, fixed his eyes upon the deck, and thus dramatically represented her condition for at least a minute.

I sought in vain in his voice, in his face, in his air, for some hint, some color, some expression of such grief of affection, of such emotion of sorrow, as the love he had spoken of as existing between them would naturally cause one to look for; instead, I seemed to find nothing but alarm, uncertainty, irritability, subdued by fear.

"We must hope," said I, "that she will speedily recover her mind."

"Will you descend into the cabin and see her ?" said he, shortly, as though he had talked this invitation over and settled it.

I was slightly startled, and answered, "What good can I do, Don Christoval ?"

"You are her countryman," said he; "your accent, that is far purer than mine when I discourse in your tongue, may excite her attention. Nor, perhaps, may it be wholly with her as I fear."

"You do not wish to imply that she is shamming ?"

He gesticulated with a fury that I could not but think pretended.

"No, no, poor girl! Shamming indeed! God defend me from conveying such an idea. But will you descend, Captain Portlack, and see her?"

"I owe the preservation of my life to you," said I, "and it is my sincere desire to be of use to you in any honest direction. But how shall I serve you by visiting madame, your wife?"

Spiritless as his eyes were, the glance he shot at me as I pronounced these words was as piercing as I had found his gaze when he inspected me on my first being taken aboard his schooner. He slightly frowned, wrenched at, rather than twirled his immense mustaches, beat softly with his foot in manifest effort to control himself, then said abruptly:

"Will you descend, Captain Portlack?"

"With pleasure," said I, and I followed him below, leaving Butler, whose watch would not expire till eight o'clock, in charge of the vessel.

Don Lazarillo was seated at the cabin table. I see him now supporting his head on his elbow, his bearded chin buried in the palm of his hand, and his finger-ends at his teeth as though he were gnawing upon his nails. He was the most perfect figure of nervous perplexity that could be imagined. He

10

looked at me swiftly, but sternly and devouringly, too, and addressed his friend in Spanish.

"Pardon me," I exclaimed, before Don Christoval could reply, "You know, gentlemen, I do not understand your tongue. This is a strange and sad affair. It will reassure me if you converse in the only speech I am acquainted with."

Don Lazarillo shrugged his shoulders.

"My friend was merely expressing satisfaction at your visit," said Don Christoval, loftily, yet without hauteur.

He turned to the door of the berth on the port or left-hand side of the schooner, hesitated as though conquering an instant's irresolution of mind, then turned the handle, motioning with his head that I should enter.

The berth was a small one. It was comfortably, almost handsomely, furnished after the style of the cabin in which the Spaniards lived; but I had no eyes just then for the equipment of the box of a place. The morning sun shone full upon the porthole, and the little room was hardly less brilliant with luster than the cabin from which I had stepped. In a low, crimson velvet arm-chair was seated the lady I had been invited to visit. She sat in the posture that had been theatrically represented to me

by Don Christoval. Her hands were locked upon
her knees, as though she had been suddenly arrested
in the act of rocking herself in a fit of wild grief;
her head was bowed, and her eyes were rooted to the
deck. I stood surveying her for some moments, but
she never stirred; she did not appear to breathe. I
did not witness the least movement of her eyes,
whose lids were fixed as though, indeed, she were a
figure of wax. She was dressed, or wrapped rather,
in a ruby-colored dressing-gown belonging, as I
might suppose by the gay style of it, to one of the
Spaniards. The collar of this gown came to her
throat. I was unable to see whether she was still
appareled in ball attire. Handsome diamond drops
hung motionless in her ears, and her hands, from
which the gloves had been removed, sparkled with
rings. There were three or four rings upon the third
finger of her left hand, but I did not observe that
one of them was a wedding ring. Her hair, that
was of a dark red and very abundant, was in great
disorder, but the remains of the wreath, which I had
noticed on her when she lay upon the sofa, had been
removed. The posture of her head left something
of her face undisclosed; what I saw of it did not
impress me as beautiful. Her eyebrows were lighter
than her hair, almost sandy; her cheeks and brow

were colorless as marble; yet her profile as I now witnessed it was not without delicacy, and I might suppose that when all was well with her she would show as a pretty woman. She looked the age Don Christoval had mentioned—twenty-two. Her stature I could not imagine, and the dressing-gown concealed her figure.

Don Lazarillo approached in a tiptoe walk and stood in the doorway staring at her.

"My dear one," said Don Christoval, faintly smiling and infusing into his accents a note of sweetness I had heard on more than one occasion in his voice, "I have brought Captain Portlack to see you. He is the captain of this schooner. He is your countryman—a true Englishman. Raise your eyes, my dear one, that you may see him," and thus speaking, with grace inexpressible, he bent his fine form over her and pressed his lips to her forehead.

Less of life could not have appeared in a statue.

"Speak to her," said Don Christoval, turning to me.

Behind us Don Lazarillo ejaculated in Spanish.

"How shall I address her?" said I, looking at the tall Spaniard.

He started, sent a glance of lightning rapidity

at his friend, reflected a moment, and then said, "Accost her as Miss Noble. By that name she may remember herself. Ay, señor, call her Ida Noble."

I bit my lip, and, planting myself by a step in front of the lady, bent my knee till my face was on a level with hers.

"Look at me, madame," said I. "I know you as Ida Noble. Look at me. I am your countryman and your *friend*."

I pronounced the word "friend" with the utmost emphasis I could communicate to it. She raised her eyes without altering the posture of her head. They were of a soft brown, and the richer for the contrast of her hair. I never could have imagined such eyes under eyebrows of so pale a yellow as hers. She looked at me during a few beats of the pulse steadfastly, and then smiled, but there was no meaning in her smile or in her regard. A moment after she bent her eyes down again, and began to sing; but the air was without music; the words which left her lips half articulated were without sense.

"Valgame Dios!" cried Don Lazarillo.

She ceased to sing and set her lips again, and continued to gaze at the deck without any signs of life, as before. I rose to my stature, and, after watching her a while, said to Don Christoval, "I can do no good."

"You made her smile, Captain Portlack," said he, in a soft whisper.

I shook my head, stepped to the door, and passed into the cabin. The others followed, Don Christoval closing the door behind him.

"I believe, with patience," said he, "that you could bring her mind back to her."

"I am no doctor, gentlemen," said I. "I know nothing about the treatment of the insane."

"What do 'ee say?" exclaimed Don Lazarillo.

"What a calamity to befall me!" cried Don Christoval, clasping his hands and upturning his face with a look of wretchedness that certainly was not counterfeited.

"Does she eat and drink?" said I.

"A little, just a little," he answered. "I put food in a plate on her knee and leave her, and when I return a little is gone."

"Should she show no signs of mending, shall you persevere in this voyage to Cuba, sir?"

"Certainly," he replied, passionately, with a gesture like a blow.

I paused to hear if he had more to say. Finding him silent, I bowed and went on deck. Butler stood at the rail abreast of the skylight. Though his face habitually carried a sulky look, owing to the sour expression into which the extremities of his mouth were curved, his was a face to assure one on the whole that its owner was a good average honest English sailor. I am not of those who believe that the character is to be read in the face: but my own experience is, that I was never yet deceived by a man to whom I had taken a liking because of his face. Yet I admit that many honest souls, many excellent hearts, go through the world with repellent countenances. Hence the unwisdom of judging by the face.

I stepped up to Butler, and looking him in the eyes I exclaimed, "Butler, I believe we have been cheated into the commission of a gallows act by the lies of those two Spaniards down below in the cabin."

His intelligence was sluggish, and he looked at me with a gaze slow of perception.

"I have just seen the lady," said I.

"Ha! and how is she a-doing, sir?"

"She is mad—undoubtedly driven mad by the outrage that has been perpetrated upon her and hers."

"Tom was saying she was off her head, and why,

'cause he heard her sing and laugh. Singing and laughing ain't no sign of madness. I asked Mariana the question plain, and he says 'No' to it—'No,' in the hearing of us all; but now you've seen her, sir, and she *is* mad?"

"She is utterly mad. Mad as from a broken heart. She sits like a figure-head, without a stir."

I paused. "She is no more Don Christoval's wife than I am," said I.

"Are you sure of that?" he cried, sharply.

"I have been almost sure of it for some time— I am quite sure of it now."

He looked as alarmed as a man with strong bushy whiskers and a skin veneered with mahogany by the weather could well appear. "How have ye made sure, Mr. Portlack?"

"She has no wedding ring."

He chewed upon this and then said: "But a wedding ring ben't no infallible sign of marriage, is it, sir? I've heered my mother say that she once lost her wedding ring and was always going to buy another, but didn't, and for years she went without a wedding ring, though father was alive most of the time, and a perticlar man, too."

"If the lady below were a married woman she would wear a wedding ring," said I.

"Ay," said he, with a knowing look entering his eyes, " but suppose the father had obliged the lady to take her wedding ring off? What more natural, seeing how he was all agin the marriage?"

To this I could return no other answer than a shake of the head. He eyed me with a small air of triumph.

"If there's nothing more to make ye doubt, Mr. Portlack," said he, "than the want of a wedding ring on the lady's finger, I'm for allowing that the Don's yarn's true."

As I had nothing more than suspicion to oppose to his desire to believe in the story, I contented myself with saying : " You will find that I am right, nevertheless. I shall go and get some breakfast, and will relieve you in ten or twelve minutes."

I walked to the main-hatch, but he followed me. "Supposing it as you say, sir," he inquired, " what 'ud be the consequences of the job to us men?"

"Transportation for life."

He muttered something under his breath and then said, "And supposing the lady to be his lawful wife, sir?"

"I am no lawyer," I answered, and dropped through the hatch.

CHAPTER VI.

A TRAGEDY.

I WAS prepared to find that Butler had carried my words forward. I returned to the deck after breakfast, and the man trudged to the forecastle, and not long afterward I observed the four seamen, the fifth being at the helm, engaged in earnest conversation. They talked, pipe in mouth, their hands deep buried in their capacious breeches pockets, and sometimes they talked with their backs upon one another, and sometimes they would pace the deck, passing one another, but always talking, and frequently they directed their eyes aft, insomuch that I expected every minute that the whole group would approach me and oblige me to share in the discussion.

My manner and my words when I had visited madame below had been altogether too pronounced for so shrewd an intelligence as that of Don Christoval to miss the true meaning of. In short, I had as good as said that I did not consider the lady to be his wife; that she had been abducted—ferociously and inhumanly stolen from her father's home, and that we Englishmen who formed his crew had been betrayed into an act of criminal villiany by his rascally lies. All this I was conscious I had as good as said, because, meaning it, I had looked it, and, in a sentence, I had suggested it. I therefore concluded that the two Spaniards would talk this matter of my suspicions over, decide upon some prompt course of action, and come to me on deck—but what to do and what to say? Would Don Christoval *admit* the adventure to be one of abduction, pleading the necessity of representing himself as married that he might obtain the assistance of English seamen, since it was clear that he would not ship Spanish sailors for the expedition; or would he approach me with threats, defying me to disprove his statement that the lady below was his wife, and giving me to understand that if I did not mind my own business——

My mind was rambling in speculations of this kind when I heard the sound of a guitar and a voice singing. The skylight lay open; I heard it as distinctly as though I were in the cabin. Don Lazarillo sat smoking at the table, keeping time with his fingers, the rings upon them sparkling as he tapped.

It was not he who was playing the guitar and singing; therefore it was Don Christoval. The sounds came from the after-part of the interior, and I had no doubt whatever that madame's door was open, and that Don Christoval was touching the strings and lifting up his voice with some quite superstitious or quite rational hope of exorcising the demon of madness out of the girl by the bewitching music he was making.

Bewitching it was. I listened, wholly fascinated by it. His voice was a clear, sweet, most thrilling and lovely tenor, soft and yet penetrating, and controlled, so far as I could possibly judge, by the most exquisite art. Whether he had ever before produced his guitar I can not say; certainly this was the first time I had heard the sound of it. He sang several airs; one of them so haunted me that I remember long afterward humming it over to a friend of mine who was a very good musician in his way, and he instantly pronounced it a composition of Mozart, giving it an Italian name which I have forgotten. I should never have supposed that music possessed the magic claimed for it until I heard that sweet, thrilling tenor voice, threaded by the tones of the delicately-touched guitar. The songs in succession wrought a fairy atmosphere for the senses.

The schooner melted out—the ocean vanished. I
was transported to a land sweet with the aroma of
the orange grove, romantic with Moorish palaces,
melodious with the laughter of dancers and the
merry rattle of the castanets.

Bless me, thought I, as I paced the deck afresh
when the singing was ended, a man need not go to
sea to visit distant countries when he may travel
farther than sail or steam can convey him by sitting
at home and listening to a tenor voice accompanied
by a guitar.

Half an hour later the two Spaniards made their
appearance. I had marked the hideous cook steal
to the companion-way, and judged that he was keeping watch. The two Dons, with lighted cigars in
their mouths, walked the deck arm-in-arm. Don
Christoval seemed to notice that the men forward
were observing him with unusual attention. I
assumed this because I perceived that he suddenly
put on an air of carelessness, of ease, even of gayety,
such as certainly was not visible in him when he
first showed himself. This air I further remarked
was swiftly copied by his companion, but on *him* it
sat with a horrible awkwardness. He had neither
the figure, the beauty, nor the skill to act as his
friend did.

Would Don Christoval challenge me for my suspicions? If so, I should be honest with him; tell
him in unmistakable English what my conviction
was; inform him that I would no longer share in
the dastardly crime into which he had betrayed his
sailors; and insist that I should be transshipped to
the first vessel that passed, or that I should be suffered to carry the schooner close enough to a coast,
the nearest at hand, to enable me to get ashore. It
was likely enough that my full mind showed in my
face. A few times I caught him eyeing me askance,
but, beyond calling out some commonplace to me
about the weather, the progress of the schooner,
and so forth, he said nothing.

It was, however, clear to me that, let his
thoughts be what they would, he could say nothing.
I was the only navigator aboard the vessel; he was
entirely at my mercy, therefore; he would rightly
fear that any menaces, any bullying, any tall-talk,
must only result in causing me to sullenly throw
up my command; in which case the schooner would
be but a little less helpless than were she reduced
to the condition of a sheer hulk by a gale of wind.

At noon I took an observation. Butler came aft
to relieve me, and I went to my quarters to work out
my sights. When I had worked out my sights and

found out the position of the schooner on the chart,
I lighted a pipe and sat down to reflect. I was now
so perfectly sure that the unhappy young lady in
the cabin had been kidnapped that my thoughts
were never for an instant influenced by the consideration that there *might* be a probability of the
Spaniard's story proving true. Everything pointed
to this expedition as an adventure of abduction.
The sailors affirmed that the girl was bleeding and
insensible when carried through the hall past the
room in which two of them with drawn cutlasses
were guarding her father and brother. This, then,
signified that she had been forcibly seized, and the
state of her apparel and the scratches upon her
shoulder proved that there had been a struggle.
Would she have struggled had Don Christoval been
her husband, to whom she was yearning to be re-
united?

My blood felt hot in my veins when I thought
upon this outrage; when I reflected how I had
been made a party to this deed of villainy; how I,
as an Englishman, had been courted by a cunning,
clever lie to abet the stealing of a countrywoman
of my own from her father's home in England by
a brace, as I might take them, of unprincipled
Spanish adventurers.

Now, while I thus sat musing over my position, and considering what course to shape to carry me clear of the dangerous association into which misadventure had brought me, I was startled by a cry in the adjacent cabin—a cry sharp, abrupt, terrible: affecting the ear as a lightning flash affects the eye. The pipe I was about to raise to my lips was arrested midway. I believe I am no coward, yet I must own that that cry, that penetrating cry, seemed to thicken my blood, seemed to stop the pulsation of my heart.

But the pause with me was brief. I dashed down my pipe, sprang to the bulk-head door and flung it open. And now what a picture did I see! The tall, commanding figure of Don Christoval was in the act of sinking to the deck; his hand was upon the table, but the fingers were slowly slipping from the edge of it, and, even as I looked, the man without a sound fell at his length and lay motionless. In the doorway of the port or left-hand berth stood the lady whom I have heretofore styled Madame, but whom I will henceforth call Ida Noble. She grasped a knife in her hand—a long carving knife it seemed to me, and I remember noticing a red gleam in it as the vessel rolled, slipping the sunshine out of a mirror toward where the girl was. She stood erect, with her eyes fixed upon the body of the Spaniard; she was as stirless as he; the figures of them both at that instant might have passed as a brace of posture-makers representing a tragedy in one of those drawing-room performances called *tableaux vivants*. Behind a chair on the starboard side of the table crouched the figure of Mariana. He squatted, and his attitude was exactly that of a monkey. His face was green; his wide-open eyes disclosed twice the usual surface of eyeball; his features were convulsed with terror, and never yet was there an artist whose imagination could have reached to the height of that fellow's hideousness, as he crouched, stabbed also, as I then believed, though this was not so.

A mad woman grasping a long knife is a formidable object; much more formidable is she when that knife is stained with blood, and when the person she has slain is still in view, lying a corpse a little distance away from her. On my showing myself, Mariana cried out, but whether in Spanish or English I knew not. What was I to do? What would you do were you suddenly confronted by a mad woman armed with a long knife? I looked up at the skylight and saw the horror-stricken countenance of Don Lazarillo peering down; but even

11

as my eye went in a glance to the Spaniard's livid face, one of the sailors, and then another of the sailors, came to his side. Count twenty, and the time you will occupy in doing so will comprise the period from the moment of my opening the door to look out down to this instant.

Next moment the girl threw the knife on the deck with a gesture of abhorrence, courtesied with irony to the body of Don Christoval, and closed the door of the berth upon herself. Then there was a rush. We could all find our courage now. Mariana sprang from behind his chair, overturning it; Don Lazarillo, followed by the two sailors, came in a few bounds through the companion-hatch. I stepped to the side of Don Christoval's body, and stood looking upon him. Stone dead I knew him to be. In Calcutta during a cholera outbreak, and on board an emigrant ship visited with fever, I had many a time stood beside the dying and the dead, and the spectacle of death was very familiar to me.

"Lock her door!" shrieked Don Lazarillo.

One of the seamen picked up the knife and viewed it at arm's length. I carefully turned the body over.

"Ay, there it is," said I, pointing to a cut slightly stained with blood in the Spaniard's waistcoat. The wound was in the left ribs, and one had but to glance at the knife to cease to wonder that the man should have dropped dead.

"Lock the door!" again shrieked Don Lazarillo in his broken English, looking from the body of his friend to the door, and from the door to the body of his friend, and recoiling, and shrinking and hugging himself, and so munching his lips that one watched to see froth upon them—doing all this as he looked.

Mariana repeatedly crossed himself, uttering all sorts of Spanish ejaculations in a voice like the subdued low of a calf.

"Is he dead, sir?" asked one of the sailors.

"He can never be more dead," said I, stooping to look into the face of the body. "They drove her mad, and this is how she requites them. A cruel, bloody business, my lads. Fling that knife overboard."

The fellow launched it javelin-fashion through an open porthole. Don Lazarillo began to scream out in Spanish. His meaning might have some reference to securing the lady; I do not know.

"Silence!" I roared. "Do you want to be the next victim?" and in my wrath I made an infuriate gesture as of stabbing; on which, with one wild

look at me, he fled up the companion steps and remained above, viewing us through the skylight.

Butler and another seaman, both very pale, and
fetching their breath quickly, entered the cabin and
looked at the body.

"Here's a murdering job to happen!" said
Scott.

"Who's done this?" cried Butler, who had
been somewhere forward when Don Christoval's
wild death-shriek had sounded.

Mariana, with a paralytic gesture, pointed to
Miss Noble's berth.

"Who's done it?" repeated Butler, in a voice
strong and hoarse with horror.

"The girl whom these Spaniards have driven
mad," said I. I turned to Mariana. "Did you see
Don Christoval stabbed?"

"Ah, Dios! yes," he answered; and in language which is to be as little conveyed as his voice,
or the expressions which chased his face, which at
every instant gave a new character to his ugliness,
he contrived to make us understand this: that
Don Christoval had entered the lady's room, where
he, Mariana, heard him address her soothingly;
that the door was suddenly flung open, and that,
at the same moment, even as the Spaniard stood

on the threshold, the girl buried the knife in his side.

"How did she come by the knife?" cried Butler.

Mariana, trembling violently, with his eyes fixed upon the door of Miss Noble's berth, as though at every moment he expected to behold it thrown open, made us understand that the negro boy, some time during the morning, had left a basket of the cabin cutlery upon the table, and that the girl must have looked out and possessed herself of a knife at some moment when the two Spaniards were on deck, and when he—Mariana—had quitted his post of sentry to enter Don Christoval's berth. This was conjecture on the fellow's part, but beyond doubt it was accurate.

Don Lazarillo continued to gaze at us through the skylight with an expression as of a horrible sneer upon his face. I again stooped over the form of Don Christoval, felt his pulse, and examined his half-closed, fast-glazing eyes, then bade a couple of the seamen pick the body up and convey it to the cabin the Spaniard had occupied. While this was doing, I grasped the handle of the door of Miss Noble's room.

"Mind!" shrieked Don Lazarillo from above. Mariana ran on deck. I felt the idleness of announcing myself by knocking. More knives than one it was possible she might have concealed; I therefore at first held the door but a little way open and looked in.

The girl was standing beside the bunk or sleeping-shelf; her elbows were upon the edge of it, her cheeks in her hands, and she stood motionlessly gazing, as I might suppose, through the port-hole. She was robed as in the morning; that is to say, in a crimson dressing-gown, which, in that era of short skirts, clothed her to her heels. She was but a little above the average stature of woman, though she had looked far taller than she really was when she stood in the doorway grasping the knife, with her eyes upon the dead Spaniard.

Finding her unarmed, I entered, carefully sweeping the room as I did so with my eyes for any signs of a knife or other weapon. The four seamen stood in the doorway, and she did not turn her head. I approached her, keeping a distance of some two or three feet between us, and prepared, poor lady! for any act of violence. Still she continued to stare through the port-hole.

"Miss Noble," said I, " you smiled at me this morning. Look at me now. You will remember me as your friend."

She turned her head slowly; not more mechanical could have been that extraordinary movement had clock-work produced it. When her soft brown eyes—in which assuredly I witnessed nothing of that sparkle or fire of madness which is said to burn in the vision of the insane—were upon me, she frowned and bit her under lip, exposing her small white front teeth. I believed from her expression that she was struggling with her memory. She then suddenly turned fully round, as though sensible of being watched from the door, and the sailors, to the wild look she gave them, stirred and fell back with uneasy shuffling motions of their feet. She stared at them for a while, and afterward at me, preserving her frown, and holding her lip under her teeth; she was deadly white, but spite of her frown, which you would have thought must give an expression of disdain or anger or contempt to her brow, her face was meaningless. She eyed me fixedly for some moments, then, with the former slow motion of her head, resumed her first posture. I stepped to the door.

"What is to be done?" said I.

"It's a cruel business. The Spaniard's been rightly sarved out," exclaimed one of the sailors.

"What is to be done?" I repeated; for here, to

be sure, was a condition of ocean life that had never
before been encountered by my experience.

The men gazed at the girl in silence. I mused,
and presently said, "One of you keep this door;
the rest of us must turn to and search the cabin, to
make sure there is nothing in it with which she can
hurt herself."

There were four of us, and there being little to
examine, we had soon satisfied ourselves that there
was no weapon anywhere hidden. She took not
the least notice of us; but when I explored her
sleeping-berth, upon whose edge, as I have told you,
her elbows reposed, she fell back a step or two, and
then, going to the arm-chair, seated herself, clasping
her knees and rooting her eyes to the deck.

"Will she have a knife about her?" said Butler,
in a hoarse whisper.

I thoroughly considered this, and, after a narrow scrutiny of her, decided that she had not concealed a knife upon her, and I was the more willing
to believe so because I had not the heart—I will
not say the courage—to search her. It shocked me
to think of offering any violence to the poor girl,
and violence I knew it must come to—she would
resist, a struggle would increase her madness—if I
laid my hands upon her. But I was certain she had

not concealed a knife. The dressing-gown she wore
was without a pocket. The sleeves were loose, and
while she stood at the bunk I had noticed that her
arms, whose wrists were still clasped by bracelets,
were bare, whence I concluded that the dressing-gown
concealed the ball attire she had been brought aboard
in. So I decided that she had not secreted a weapon, because, recollecting her attire as she lay upon
the sofa in the cabin after she had been brought to
the schooner, I could not conceive that it offered
any points for the concealment of a knife.

I closed the door upon her, and we stood outside
consulting. Our debate determined us to this:
that while she continued in this passive condition
she was to be left as she was; that for the present
the five seamen would take it turn and turn about
to watch that she did not quit her room; that she
was to be fed as heretofore, that is to say, food
and wine were to be placed before her, of which
she would partake if she chose, for no man could
compel her to eat. Then, no longer choosing that
the helmsman should remain alone on deck—for
Don Lazarillo, Mariana, and the negro boy counted
for nothing—I went to the companion steps and
was followed by Butler and two others.

Don Lazarillo and Mariana stood a little way

forward of the skylight. They conversed, and
their gestures expressed unbounded horror and dis-
may. On our appearing, they fell silent and
watched us. Some distance beyond them was the
figure of the negro boy. There was nothing in
sight. The white canvas soared round and brilliant,
and the rigging was vocal with the gushing of the
blue breeze. Astern of us ran an arrowy wake of
foam, and off the weather bow rose a steady sound
of seething, like to the noise made by the boiling
foot of a cataract heard afar.

I took up a position near the tiller, that was in
the grasp of the seaman Tubb, and the sailors stood
near me.

" What's happened below ? " said Tubb.

" The tall Spaniard's been stabbed dead by the
mad lady," answered South.

Tubb delivered himself of a long whistle, following it on by an agitated swing of the tiller that
hove the schooner to the wind two points before he
could recover her.

"And now what is to be done ? " said I. " You
see the pass we've been brought into. Two men
dead of the adventure, and the rest of us guilty of
a deed that must earn us transportation for life
should the law get hold of us. What's to be done,

I say? Is this voyage to Cuba to be prosecuted? Our duty is—and let me tell you our policy is—to make all the restitution that is possible, and that we can alone do by conveying the poor lady home."

"I ain't going home," cried Butler in a voice of obstinacy, smiting his thigh.

Don Lazarillo and Mariana crept, or sneaked rather, by a pace nearer to us and stood listening.

"And *I* ain't going home," said Tubb, fetching the head of the tiller a whack. "You talk of transportation for life, Mr. Portlack; d'ye want it to happen, sir?"

"No," I answered; "but I wish to do what is right, and to make it as right as right can be by doing it quickly. The lady must be restored to her friends."

"No offense, Mr. Portlack," said Scott, "but we aren't to forget that you're on the right side of the hedge. You wasn't in the mellee; we was. Your going home can't sinnify; ourn means lagging for all hands."

The two Spaniards sneaked a little closer.

"I wish to suggest nothing likely to imperil you," said I. "Though I was never willingly of you—you don't want me to tell you how it happens that I'm here; yet being of you, you'll find me with

you, content to share in all that may befall you.
As to my being on the right side of the hedge,"
cried I, rounding upon Scott, "that's but a notion
of yours. The lawyers may think very much
otherwise. But I say this, that since these two
Spaniards have decoyed our heads into a noose,
the only way to avoid being strangled is to whip
our heads out again; and d'ye ask how that's to be
done? My answer is, Do what is right. Act so
that you'll be able to say, should you come to be
charged as helpers in this crime of abduction:
We believed the lady to be the Spaniard's wife; we
were told that a man had a right to his own, and
we were willing to help him to his own, but the
moment we found we had been deceived we turned
to like honest men, to make all the amends in our
power by restoring the poor lady to her friends.
That is what's in my head, and it is the advice I
give you, and wish you to act upon for my sake and
for yours."

South looked thoughtfully at Butler; but Butler,
with an angry countenance, vengefully smiting his
thigh again with his clinched fist, cried out,
"There's to be no going home with me. There's
to be no taking the chance of the law with me.
There's to be no risking even a week o' jail with

me. Ye may call it Cuba, or ye may call it
Madagascar, but let no man speak of the United
Kingdom. I've got my liberty, and I'm for keeping of it. 'Sides," he whipped out, " who's going
to pay me my money, now the Spaniard as hired us
is dead and gone ? "

The eyes of the men at this were at once bent
upon Don Lazarillo.

"Sooner than go home I'd start away in that
there boat," said Scott, pointing to the cutter on
the main deck, "and take my chance of making the
land or being picked up. I once had a fortnight of
quod for refusing to sail after joining. That was
enough for me. No more, thank ye." He stepped
to the rail and violently expectorated.

"Who's going to pay us?" said Trapp. " If
t'others are of my mind, there'll be no leaving this
schooner till we've received every farden of our
money. We've earnt it, by ——— !" he added, hitting
the tiller head another thump.

"Mr. Portlack," said Butler, gazing at me
gloomily and mutinously, "you still talk as if you
was cocksure that the lady wasn't the tall gent's
wife."

I paused while I gazed at him, then, with vehement strides, walked up to Don Lazarillo.

"You and your dead friend," I cried, staring into the shrinking and working face of the man, "have cheated me and the men here by your lies into the commission of a crime. You know," I thundered, determined to terrorize him into a confession of the truth, "that the poor lady below, whom you have driven mad, was not Don Christoval's wife. Dare to tell me she was, you villain, and I'll fling you overboard!"

"What ees it you say?" he cried, with his swarthy face of the color of pepper with fear.

"*You* understand me!" I shouted, addressing Mariana. "You have been in the secret, too, from the beginning. Own it, you dog, own it, or I'll throttle you."

I raised my hand; the ugly creature delivered a singular cry and dropped on his knees.

"Señor Portlack," he whined, "spare my life, for the blessed Virgin's sake, and if I do not tell you the truth may Satan catch my soul now and carry it away to eternal torment. The señorita was not the cavalier's wife. The caballero's story was true in all but that part. She was the lady of his love, but not his wife. If I'm not speaking the truth, may my soul be tormented for ever and ever." Saying which he crossed himself and stood up.

The obligation of feigning wrath alone pre-
served me from bursting into a laugh at the sight
of his hideous face convulsed with fear.

"Explain to Don Lazarillo," cried I, sternly,
"what you have told me."

He did so. Don Lazarillo watched him with
sparkling eyes and ashen cheek, and on his ceasing
made as if he would strike him.

"Will you deny that Mariana speaks the truth?"
I exclaimed.

The Spaniard shot at me a look of mingled
malice, hate, and fright, then, with a shrug of the
shoulders that convulsed his figure, he turned his
back, and, with clasped hands, stood viewing the
ocean over the rail.

"Now, men," said I, addressing Butler and the
others, "you have heard the truth for yourselves, and
you may read it also in that Spanish gentleman's
behavior. Isn't it abominable that we Englishmen,
or let me say that *you* Englishmen, should have
been tricked by the lies of a brace of foreigners
into helping them to steal a poor young lady of
your own country from her father's home? For
what purpose was this done? There was little
enough love in it, I'll swear. She is no doubt an
heiress, and the Don that lies dead below hoped,

by stealing her, to steal her fortune also; and you
may take it that yonder gentleman," I continued,
pointing at Don Lazarillo, "entered upon this inhuman undertaking as a speculation. That's my
notion, and if he understands what I'm saying, he
knows that I've hit the truth. He was to share
in the plunder, on condition of his finding money
enough to equip this expedition."

My eyes rested upon Mariana as I spoke; the
ugly rascal, to whom my words seemed perfectly
intelligible, let his head sink, in an affirmative
gesture. The wretch, in fact, was horribly fright-
ened, feared for his life, in short, and by the looks
of him I might not only know that he was willing
to tell all, but to tell more than all, to appease my
wrath, which I must own was largely simulated.

Butler stepped up to Don Lazarillo, whose back
was still upon us, and touched the man's elbow
with his forefinger.

"Here," said he, "what about my money?"

Don Lazarillo appeared deaf, and continued to
stare over the rail. Butler thrust at his elbow again
with his long forefinger.

"I am asking," he said, "about my money.
Who's a-going to pay me?"

The other seamen now drew close to the Spaniard, who stood as though deaf. Mariana rapidly and hoarsely uttered a sentence or two in Spanish, probably a translation of Butler's words. Don Lazarillo then whipped round; his eyes glowed like live coals, but his ashy pallor was more defined than before. On finding himself confronted by the three sailors, he placed himself in the posture of a man at bay with a sword in his hand, only, happily, he was without a sword.

"What do you want?" he cried.

"Who's a-going to pay us?" shouted Butler, unnecessarily exerting his lungs, as the custom is with us English when we address foreigners, whose incapacity to understand seems to suggest deafness to our insular minds.

Don Lazarillo, looking toward me, exclaimed, "I speak about dat wiz ze Capitan Portlack."

"Ay," cried Scott, "but if you can talk to him, you can talk to us. It's we that's consarned. It's us as wants to know who's a-going to pay us. You've brought us into a blooming mess with your lies, and the five of us men, as Captain Dopping shipped at Cadiz, stands for to be transported if so be as our law catches hold of us, and all along of you and him as lays below. If you can talk to Mr. Portlack, you can talk to us."

12

"What you weesh me say?" cried the miserable Spaniard, extending his arms, and casting a look of entreaty at me.

"Who's a-going to pay us men?" vociferated Butler, striking the palm of his left hand with a leg-of-mutton fist. The men stood so close to Don Lazarillo that he was forced to dodge his head here and there to catch a sight of Mariana, to whom he cried out something in his native tongue.

"Señor Portlack," said the cook, in a cringing attitude, "Don Lazarillo beg me say he will speak wid you. I will translate."

"Let it be so, men," I exclaimed; "you'll do no good by shouting questions to a man who doesn't understand you."

They drew away sulkily. Don Lazarillo pulled off his hat to pass a large colored silk handkerchief over his forehead. He then stepped up to me. The cook posted himself close to him, and the sailors, with whom now was the negro boy, took up a station within easy earshot. Mariana translating, the dialogue took this form :—

"The men wish to know who is to pay them their wages?"

"Don Christoval is now dead," answered the Spaniard. "This adventure therefore terminates!"

"How?—terminates?" I cried. "We are still upon the high seas. We have still the young lady with us to restore to those from whom you and your friend stole her. No, no, this adventure has not yet terminated!"

"What do you mean to do?" he asked.

"That is no answer to my question. Who will pay those men for the work they have done, the risks they have run, and have yet to run?"

He put his hand to his brow, and, after a pause, said, "I must think."

The sailors fell a-shouting exclamations. The chorus was swelled by the voices of the man at the helm, and by the fellow below, who had got upon the cabin table, and stood with his head in the open skylight, listening.

"Silence!" I cried; "how am I to transact your business if you interrupt me? The men," I continued, addressing the Spaniard, "look to you for payment. They will not lose sight of you until you pay them. Have you money with you, or the equivalent of money?" I added, fixing my eyes upon his rings and brooch; "for *I* must be paid, Don Lazarillo, and *they* must be paid."

"I will answer. I will be honorable. I will give my word; and the word of a Spanish gentle-

men is gold." A growl proceeded from the seamen. "But first, as a matter of courtesy, to help
my mind in its blindness—for the death of my
friend has caused my brains to spin round in my
head—I entreat you, señor, to tell me what are
your intentions?"

"To restore the young lady to her friends."

"What!" he cried, shouting the words with a
face of horror to Mariana; "you will proceed to
England?"

I responded with a vehement nod.

"Then vot sall become of me?" he exclaimed in
English.

I shrugged my shoulders. He folded his arms
tightly upon his breast, and, with bowed head, fell
to measuring a few feet of the deck. We all
watched him in silence while he thus walked. Suddenly he stopped, and, turning upon Mariana, addressed him volubly and with amazing energy,
making a very windmill of his arms. I knew that
he was saying a great deal more than Mariana could
translate, more, indeed, to judge from the expression that entered the cook's face, than the repulsive-
looking creature would choose to translate. Nevertheless, I waited in patience, making a single gesture
of command to the sailors to be still.

Mariana then spoke; the substance of his speech was this: Don Lazarillo asked for a few hours. He desired to look over the effects of his dead friend; he desired time to mature a proposal which he hoped to make to me. This was substantially all that Mariana translated. Yet, owing to his slow delivery and to his broken-winded English, the matter he delivered appeared to contain much more than was in it. I had no doubt, however, that Don Lazarillo in his speech had acquainted the fellow with some half-formed scheme in his mind, as good for Mariana perhaps as for himself.

I told the cook to inform the Don that we would give him until six o'clock that evening, and that if he was not ready with his proposals by that hour, I should shift the schooner's helm for England, where, on my arrival, it would be my duty to deliver him and Mariana into the hands of justice. The cook, in translating this, was almost as ashen in color as the other.

Don Lazarillo descended into the cabin. Butler came up to me.

"You're merely frightening the man, I hope, sir," said he, "with this here talk of sailing to England?"

"Let's settle with him first," I answered, "and

then I'll call a council of the crew. Meanwhile it is senseless to keep the schooner under all this canvas. Let us shorten sail and lay her with her head to the east until we hear what Don Lazarillo has to say for himself."

He looked doubtfully round the sea, then consented. So we reduced the schooner down to what is termed a scandalized mainsail and a jib, and all that afternoon she lay under that canvas, blowing along very quietly eastward.

Some time about four o'clock I went below and asked Trapp, who was still on watch in the cabin, if all had been quiet in the lady's cabin.

"Ne'er so much noise as a mouse would have made, sir," said he.

I lightly tapped on the young lady's door, and without waiting for a response, which I knew I should not obtain, I turned the handle and looked in. The girl was seated in her chair, but her head lay back upon the cushioned round of it. Her eyes were sealed, and her lips apart. I looked at her, scarcely knowing whether she was alive or dead; but presently observing that her bosom rose and fell, I went to her side, put my ear to her mouth, and heard her breathing regularly and peacefully. I stood a while looking at her, my heart full of pity. I peered closely at her fingers: her rings were rich and beautiful—diamonds and rubies of great value; but I might make sure now there was no wedding-ring buried among the three or four which armored the finger the ring would have been on. One little foot showed, and I perceived that she was shod with white satin. There was something to shock me in the ironic contrast created by the sight of that satin shoe—the contrast between the grim and tragic reality that was now hers and the festal vision of the ball-room, with its swimming figures, the bright music of the dance, the gleam of fans, the scent of flowers.

I was happy to discover that she was able to sleep. It seemed to my plain mind a good sign, for I had often been told that sleeplessness was one of the horrible conditions of insanity; that not to be able to sleep drove men mad; and that when they were mad still they were sleepless. Strange as it will seem, I could not, I did not, associate any horror of assassination with that restful figure. I had seen her standing at the door, and had marked the red gleam upon the knife she held; I had seen the tall and handsome Spaniard in the act of falling, then tumbling his whole length and expiring. Yet I could gaze at this poor girl without the least emotion of aversion, without the least sense of that sort of horrid unaccountable fascination with which red-handed crime constrains the gaze of the spectator.

This was not, I think, because I knew she was mad, and, being mad, irresponsible, and, being irresponsible, virtually guiltless. No; it was because of a singular atmosphere of purity and sweetness about her as she now lay sleeping. Beautiful she was not. Indeed, she was not even what might be called pretty; but now that she slept the demon within her slept also. What was native in her showed in her countenance. You witnessed it in this slumber of madness as you would have beheld it in her waking hours of sanity. I stood viewing her and I thought to myself she is a refined lady, pure, gentle, and good.

CHAPTER VII

I WENT out, closing the door behind me, and called to Butler through the skylight to send the negro boy to me. The lad arrived, and I bade him prepare a tray of refreshments for Miss Noble.

"How does the poor lady do, sir?" said Trapp, who sat in a chair looking on while I got upon the table and called.

"She is sound asleep," said I. "So much the better. You can go forward and get your supper. I'll keep a look-out here for the present."

He went away, and presently the boy Tom arrived with the tray, on which he had heaped some cold ham, fruit, jelly from a bottle, and so forth. I poured some wine into a tumbler, and softly entering the lady's berth placed the tray beside her on the deck, where, should the schooner begin to frisk, it would slide without capsizing. I supposed that all this while Don Lazarillo was in his own

cabin gnawing, as his trick was, upon his finger-
ends while he reflected upon the proposals he was
presently to submit. My thoughts went from him
to his dead friend, and I stepped to the berth where
the body lay to look at it.

On opening the door I beheld Don Lazarillo on
his knees at the side of the bunk in which reposed
the body of Don Christoval. His hands were
clasped, his eyes were upturned, and, though his
accents were inaudible outside the door, he prayed
with so much fervor as to be for some moments
insensible of my presence. Then bringing his flash-
ing eyes from the upper deck he directed them at
me, made the sign of the cross upon his breast, rose
to his feet, made the sign of the cross upon the face
of the dead body, on whose breast he had laid a
crucifix, and then looked at me.

I went to the side of the bunk and stood for a
few moments gazing at the pale, still, serene, most
handsome face of the dead.

"When ees he to bury?" said Don Lazarillo.

"To-night," said I.

"He is Catolique," he exclaimed.

"We shall have to cast him into the sea without
ceremony, I fear," said I, "unless you will say
some prayers over him."

He seemed to understand me, for he nodded eagerly, and then, as if to an afterthought, made me a very low, humble bow of thanks. Pointing to my fingers, then to the chain of my watch, and then to the body of the Spaniard, I said, " Will you see to his property ? "

He pulled open a drawer and motioned me to observe some objects wrapped in a silk pocket-handkerchief. On this I looked again at the body, and now saw that the one or two rings and other jewelry which Don Christoval had worn were removed. I walked out of the berth, leaving Don Lazarillo to proceed with his prayers, earnestly hoping, however, that he would be ready with his proposals by six o'clock, and that they would be practicable and consistent with my own wishes ; because if he made no sign I should be at a loss, since it was certain that the crew would not suffer me to execute my threat to carry him to England while they remained on board ; and how to deal with *them* was a problem I should not very well be able to solve until I had dealt with *him*.

I told Tom to procure me a cup of chocolate from Mariana. I then took a cigar from a locker in which were many boxes of cigars, and, seating myself in an arm-chair, smoked and ruminated on

the tragic incidents of the day. Shortly before six
I peeped into Miss Noble's room. She still slept
soundly, exactly in the posture in which I had left
her. This I did not think wonderful, since, for all
I knew, she might not have slept a wink while she
had been aboard the schooner, and nature, utterly exhausted, had claimed at last the heavy arrears owing
to her. I listened: her breathing was perfectly
placid; her bosom rose and fell gently and regularly. I touched her hand and found it warm. The
refreshments were upon the deck untouched, as I
had placed them.

As I closed the door upon the sleeping girl,
Don Lazarillo emerged from the cabin in which
his friend's remains lay. There was a scowl upon
his face that darkened his cheeks like a deeper dye
of complexion. I watched him out of the corners
of my eyes, saying to myself, " This man is a
Spaniard; I have used strong words to him; he
would think nothing of serving me as Miss Noble
served his friend." He drew a paper cigar from
a pocket case, lighted it, and sat down, pointing
to the little clock in the skylight as he did so, as
though he would say, " You see I am punctual."
And, in truth, it was exactly six o'clock.

He broke the silence by making me understand

that he wished for Mariana. The sailors were assembled at the skylight gazing down impatiently, and I bade one of them tell the cook to lay aft, and for Butler and two others to join us below.

"But come quietly," said I, "and make no noise when you're here, for Miss Noble is asleep. One of you must remain on deck to keep a look-out."

This fell to George South, and Andrew Trapp was at the helm. Butler, Scott, and Tubb came below, and they were hastily followed by Mariana. The conversation (as translated by the cook, though it is needless, perhaps, to say that my version is somewhat more intelligible than the original as it appeared in Mariana's speech) proceeded thus:

"Well, Don Lazarillo," said I, "you have had plenty of time to consider. What now do you wish to say?"

"La Casandra is my property," he replied; "she is owned by me, and I placed her at the disposal of Don Christoval del Padron. You talk of carrying her to England. I do not wish that she should go to England."

"It is my business to restore the young lady to her friends," said I; "and since this schooner carried her off from them, most assuredly she will have to carry her back to them."

" But what is to become of my schooner when you have her in England ? "

" I do not know, and I do not care," said I. " Stop ! I will tell you this: I shall hand her over to the shipping authorities at the port at which we arrive. I will name you as her owner. You can claim her, if you will, but I shall be compelled to tell the story of this adventure, and to explain the part you took in it."

" What's all this got to do with paying of us ? " growled Butler.

Don Lazarillo sat scowling at me.

" You are quite at liberty," I continued, " to remain on board your own schooner ; but in that case you return with us to England, where certainly my immediate duty will be to inform against you."

He snarled a malediction.

" What about our money ? Ask him that," cried Scott to Mariana.

" I will send you and the lady," said Don Lazarillo, " to the first passing ship that is proceeding to England, and these sailors will continue the voyage with me to Cuba."

" Who's going to navigate the vessel ? " said Tubb.

" A passing ship will help us to a lieutenant," answered Don Lazarillo.

"Where's the passing ship to come from?" sneered Butler. "Who's a-going to wait for her? And d'ye think us men 'ud be content to mess about in this blooming schooner, may be for weeks, not knowing where we are and not knowing how to head? Ask the gent who's a-going to pay us, cook? That's what we're assembled for to hear."

"Besides," said I, "I should not dream of transferring Miss Noble to another vessel in her present condition."

I spied Don Lazarillo and Mariana exchanging a look. Indeed, I already more than suspected that these proposals of the Spaniards so far were no more than a "try on," to use a cant term; that he held another card in his hand ready to play should he be forced to do so, but that, meanwhile, his business was to make the best terms he could for himself. This conjecture was confirmed by the next speech of his that Mariana translated:

"Then what remains but for me to be transshipped to a passing vessel—Mariana and me?"

"That is reasonable. That shall be done," said I. "It is what I myself should have proposed."

"*Contento!*" said Don Lazarillo, and was silent.

"What about our money?" said Butler.

The Spaniard looked round him on Mariana ren-

dering this, then said, " I will give drafts upon my
bank at Madrid."

Butler, who was clearly the sea lawyer of this
little community, fastening his eyes upon the rings
on Don Lazarillo's fingers, shook his head with a
contemptuous snort of laughter. " No, no," cried
he, " I know what drafts be. A draft's a check,
and a check's a bit of paper as may be made not
worth the ink it's wrote upon with by the party
withdrawing of his money from the bank. No,
no," he continued, shaking his head somewhat sav-
agely at Don Lazarillo, " we want money, not paper,
and if ye can't pay us in money, then ye've got to
settle with us in what is next best to it." And here
he looked significantly at the Don's rings again.

" You may tell Don Lazarillo," said I to Mariana, " that we shall not be satisfied with his drafts,
nor with anything short of the cash he may have
about him ; and what he may lack in cash he must
make good in jewelry, of which he and his dead
friend have plenty between them."

When this was interpreted, an expression like
a spasm passed over Don Lazarillo's face. He reflected, then, with a passionate gesture, whipped out
a pocket-book, from which he abstracted a handsome
gold pencil-case, and all very passionately, with

knitted brows and muttering lips, he entered certain
figures, then shrieked rather than pronounced the
amount to the cook, naming it in Spanish currency.
Mariana nodded. Don Lazarillo now addressed him
with excitement, then, springing to his feet, he entered Don Christoval's room, from which, in a few
minutes, he returned bearing with him a bag of yellow leather, and the silk pocket-handkerchief which,
as he had given me to understand, contained his de-
ceased friend's jewelry. He opened the bag with
trembling fingers, and then, with glowing eyes, he
capsized the contents on to the table. This con-
sisted of English sovereigns—two or three hundred,
I should have imagined.

"Count," shrieked the Spaniard, "and divide."

I counted, and made the sum exactly a hundred
and fifty pounds.

"Divide," yelled Don Lazarillo, and he added
some terms in Spanish which Mariana did not think
proper to interpret. The cook's eyes gleamed like
the blade of a new poniard as he looked at the
money. I told thirty pounds for each man; for
this, it seems, was the wages agreed upon for the
run. Don Lazarillo then thrust the little parcel of
jewelry which had belonged to his friend across
to me.

13

"Dat veel pay you, I hope, Capitan Portlack," he exclaimed, hooking his thumbs in the arms of his waistcoat, and leaning back with an assumption of haughtiness and contempt, which fitted him as ill as the clothes of Don Christoval would.

I opened the handkerchief, and found a handsome gold watch and chain and a very fine diamond ring. I gave Don Lazarillo a nod, and without speech put these articles into my pockets. The value of this jewelry to purchase it would probably have amounted to three or four times the sum I was to receive ; but then I estimated the things at their selling price, which probably might not reach to fifty guineas, so that in pocketing them I was taking no more than was my due.

"You are now all satisfied, I hope," exclaimed Don Lazarillo, through Mariana. Yes, we were all satisfied. "And you put Mariana and me and my effects on board the first passing ship that will receive us ? "

"Yes," said I.

"But suppose that she is sailing to Australia or to India ? "

"I shall not be able to help that," said I. "You may stay in this schooner if you please, but Miss Noble must be conveyed home."

He rose from his seat frowning, viciously bit off the end of a cigar, lighted it, and went on deck, followed by the cook.

"Well, your minds are easy now, I hope, my lads?" said I, rising.

"We're obliged to ye, Mr. Portlack," answered Butler. "You've managed first-rate for us. And now, d'ye know, sir, while I've been sitting at this table an idea's come into my head."

"What is that idea?"

"It consarns our leaving the schooner, sir."

"Let me hear it."

"There's that big boat amidships," said he. "We shipped at Cadiz, and it was known at Cadiz that this here Casandra sailed from that port on such and such a day. Now my idea is: suppose you run in for the Spanish land until you've got Cadiz within, say, half-a-day's sail. Us men will then launch the cutter and start away for the port, you giving us its bearings. We must turn to and invent a yarn and represent this schooner as having foundered, the rest of the people who got away in the small boat being lost sight of by us. There are plenty of vessels at Cadiz, and they're always in want of hands. We can ship as smartly as we choose, get away, and then there'll be an end."

I reflected, and said, " I think your scheme excellent, and Cadiz, though still somewhat south, is,
in my opinion, as good as any other port. Only,
when you are gone and the two Spaniards transshipped, I shall be alone in this schooner."

"There'll be Tom, sir," said Tubb.

I smiled.

" If you're to return to England, Mr. Portlack,"
said Butler, pronouncing his words with great
emphasis, " in this here schooner, and we're to
leave you, which must be, for ne'er a man of us
must dream of going home for a long spell to come
arter such a job as this, then what I say is, there's
no help for it. Alone ye'll have to be until such
times as a passing vessel 'ull loan ye a man or two
to help you home."

" Your scheme requires reflection," said I.
" Give me time to think over it. And now, since
you're below, you may as well turn to and get that
body yonder ready for the last toss. We'll drop it
over the side at eight bells."

I walked to Miss Noble's cabin and looked in.
She was still asleep, preserving absolutely her former posture. I beckoned to Butler, who was at
that instant stepping from Don Christoval's berth.
He approached, and I said, "See there," pointing

to the lady. "She has been sleeping like that pretty nearly ever since we left the berth after searching it."

"Is she sleeping?" said he.

"Yes," said I, "but there is something unnatural in such slumber as this. She has not stirred a finger for some hours."

"She seems breathing all right, and appears comfortable enough, sir," said he, after silently surveying her.

"She does not look comfortable. I wish to see her in her bunk. Let us gently lift her into it. If she wakens she may prove to have her mind. Observe her face; there is no madness in that placid expression."

We were both strong men, and, bending over her we grasped, swiftly raised, and laid her at her length in the bunk. She never moved. It was indeed like lifting a statue; just as we placed her so did she continue to lie, breathing quietly with an expression upon her lips that was almost a smile.

"Well," hoarsely whispered Butler, "blowed if I could ha' believed in such a thing had I been told it. She may be a-dying."

"I hope not," said I; "one would wish to right

the enormous wrong that has deen done her before she dies."

We stood in the doorway a few minutes looking at her, talking in whispers of the assassination of the Spaniard, and of other matters growing out of that tragic subject, such as the part that Don Lazarillo was playing in this extraordinary enterprise, the probability of the girl having lost her reason for life, and so forth, during which the young lady lay as motionless as though she rested in her coffin. Butler then left the cabin to obtain materials for stitching up the body in, and I went on deck.

We buried the remains of Don Christoval at eight bells that evening, that is, at eight o'clock. It was a fine moonless evening, with so much starlight in the heavens that the twilight seemed to still dwell in the atmosphere when the afterglow had long ago died out. There was a pleasant breeze, and a sullen, steady sweep of swell, over which the schooner, almost denuded of her canvas—for our plans were not yet formed—rode with the regularity of the tick of a clock.

Ever since sunset Don Lazarillo had hung about in the waist, conversing with Mariana in Spanish in subdued accents, yet with an energy that again and again ran a hiss through his utterance. The body, with a couple of cannon shot attached to its feet, was handed on deck by three of the men; it was then placed upon a piece of the main-hatch cover, and hoisted to the lee-rail, the foot of the cover resting on the rail, while the head was supported by Butler and South. The two Spaniards, who had fallen dumb when the body was brought on deck, repeatedly crossed themselves, holding their hats in their hands, while the men were manœuvring at the sides with Don Christoval's remains.

"Are you ready ?" said I.

"All ready, sir," answered Butler.

"Pull off your caps, lads," said I, and, bareheaded, I stepped up to Don Lazarillo and begged him to recite the prayers he desired to pronounce over his friend's ashes.

He responded with a bow, which, for the moment, affected me by its mixture of courtesy and grief, and then, with Mariana stalking at his heels, approached the body. They went down upon their knees, and Don Lazarillo prayed loudly, the cook occasionally striking in with an ejaculation. I gazed with respect, and even reverence, at this strange picture. No matter what a man's faith may be, no matter what his color may be, no matter how wild and grotesque the accents in which he vents himself, never can I behold him praying to the Being in whom he believes, yea, even though he be a John Chinaman prostrate to the flat of his forehead upon the floor of his joss-house, without being strangely moved and melted into feelings and sensations in which one should seem to find but little affinity with the rough life of the ocean. The Spaniard's prayers were not mine, his religion was not mine; but what signifies *that*, thought I, as I stood listening and gazing; every man sets his watch in the dark, and it is but reasonable that every man should think his own time right.

The night wind, damp with dew, hummed in the rigging; the dark water broke from the gentle thrust of the stem in sobs, while Don Lazarillo prayed, and while Mariana ejaculated. As my eye went to the pale glimmering shape of the canvas I heard again the sounds of the sweet tenor voice as it had quietly rung through the open skylight that morning. I heard again the harp-like notes of the delicately-fingered guitar. I beheld again those visions which that clear, melodious voice had evoked, those summer aromatic scenes which Don Christoval's songs had painted upon the vision of my mind. The Spaniards rose from their knees. Don

Lazarillo made the sign of the cross upon the body, then pronounced some word in Spanish, with a sob in his tone.

"Let it go, men," said I.

They tilted the hatch, and the pale shape flashed over the side.

"Is Butler forward there?" I called out as I was pacing the quarter-deck half an hour later.

"Here he is, sir," responded Butler's voice.

"Step aft," said I. He arrived. "Butler, I've been thinking over your scheme. For the last half-hour I've been thinking of nothing else. If you men go away in the boat, will the negro boy Tom be willing to remain with me?"

"Yes, sir."

"How do you know."

"I put the question to him and he said he would be willing."

"Then," I exclaimed, "I consent. I agree with you that, if you are to leave me, I must be alone until I can get help. I might indeed transship you, feign to the master of the vessel we should speak that you were mutineers—a character you would all have to support—and ask him to give me two or three men in exchange for my five. That I might do; but the business would consist of a lie, and I hate lies. We should have to act a part: the five of you would have to invent a yarn, and carefully stick to it, while you were aboard the vessel that received you. . . . No! your plan is the most straightforward, and the least troublesome. The risk is mine, and a heavy risk it is—to be left in a big vessel with one hand only, and that hand a boy, and a mad lady below, who will require watching, and who may attempt our lives when she awakes. But I see no other way out of the difficulty."

"Nor I, sir," he answered. "We don't like the notion of leaving ye alone; but then, you insist upon carrying this here schooner to England, and to England we don't mean to go," said he, slapping his leg.

"Say no more. We'll hold that matter settled. Only, before you leave, the two Spaniards must have left; otherwise they'll be cutting Tom's and my throat, taking their chance, as I shall have to take my chance, of being fallen in with and succored. The Don doesn't like the notion of losing his schooner; but lose her he must, for he'll never dare to lay claim to her."

"I should think not!" said he. "Well, sir, then I'll tell my mates it's settled. What about leaving the vessel under this small canvas?"

"Oh," I answered, "sail can now be made, and I'll shape a course for Cadiz. As we approach the land, we stand to fall in with some trader, who'll put the two Spaniards ashore on their native soil."

I was in charge of the deck, and it was for me, therefore, to give the necessary orders for sail to be made. The sailors sprang about with marvelous agility. The influence of the money they had received operated far more strongly in them than the influence of the funeral they had witnessed, and I believe that nothing had restrained them from sing- ing, dancing, making a night of it, in short—for the fellows were never without plenty of a cheap sort of claret that had been economically laid in for their consumption—nothing, I say, had hindered them from celebrating their payment of thirty pounds a man by a forecastle carousal, but the feel- ing that some trifling respect was due to the mem- ory of the dead and to the affliction of Don Laza- rillo. Sail was heaped upon the schooner. Her twin spires floated through the liquid dusk that was radiant with large trembling stars, and a sheen melted off the edges of the canvas into the gloom, as though the whole fabric were some tall island of ice.

Don Lazarillo sat under the skylight; he lay

back in his chair with his legs crossed, his hands clasped upon his waistcoat, and a long cigar forking out of his mouth. His eyes of fire were fixed upon one of the cabin lamps, and I saw them gleaming, through the clouds of smoke he expelled, like the lanterns of a light-ship on a thick night. His countenance wore an expression of desperate dejection. Some distance away from him sat the man South, whose turn it was to watch beside Miss Noble's cabin door. This duty I conceived might, for the next two hours, at all events, be intrusted to the negro boy. He was somewhere forward. I called to him, and he came along to me out of the gloom; his black face so blending with the obscurity that the white jacket and canvas breeches he wore made him resemble a body without a head.

"You are satisfied to remain with me, Tom," said I, " when the sailors leave me?"

"Yes, massa."

"You are a good boy, and a plucky boy. We shall not be long without help, I expect. I will take care that you are rewarded." The expanse of his teeth by a sudden grin was like a streak of dim light upon the darkness. "Go below into the cabin," said I, "and relieve South. Let him go forward. You know what you have to watch?"

"Dah lady's door, sah."

He descended, and up came South, who was immediately followed by Don Lazarillo. The Spaniard, temporarily blinded by the brilliance he had emerged from, stood in the companion-way staring around ; then perceiving me, he crossed the deck and with great haste and agitation addressed me in Spanish.

"No compreny, no compreny, Don Lazarillo!" I exclaimed, and sang out for Mariana to be sent aft. The fellow promptly arrived, and upon him the Don instantly discharged a whole torrent of words.

"What is wrong?" said I.

The cook answered that Don Lazarillo wished Miss Noble's cabin to be watched by a seaman. Tom was a boy. Should Miss Noble dash out of her cabin armed with a knife, what would Tom be able to do?

"Tell Don Lazarillo," said I, "that Miss Noble is slumbering in what seems to be a trance."

The Don violently shook his head. His friend had been assassinated : he himself might be the next victim. By the bones of St. Thomas, was he to be stuck in the back like a pig, or to have his head half severed from his body in his sleep? He

would ask Captain Portlack to do him a great favor
—to exchange quarters with him. He, Don Lazarillo, with Señor Portlack's courteous permission,
would sleep under the main hatch during the remainder of his stay on board La Casandra.

I promptly assented, and that the unhappy Spaniard should meanwhile enjoy some little ease of
mind, I called to South and bade him resume his
look-out in the cabin. I now hoped to be able to
get the truth about this wild and tragic expedition
out of Don Lazarillo, and, with as much tact as I
was master of, sought through Mariana to direct
the conversation that way. But I was disappointed.
Don Lazarillo returned evasive answers, and then,
suddenly complaining of the cold, made me a bow
and withdrew to the cabin with Mariana, who, I
presently ascertained, immediately went to work
to prepare my quarters for the reception of the
Don.

After ten o'clock I saw no more of the Spaniard. I had heard some sound of hammering, but
knew not what it signified until South, coming up
out of the cabin after having been relieved by one
of the seamen, informed me that it had been caused
by Mariana nailing up the bulk-head door that led
to the sleeping quarters I had occupied. "The Don

don't mean that the lady shall get at him, sir," said the man, with a short laugh.

I stepped into the cabin to mix myself a glass of grog, dim the lamps, and take a look round.

"Has all been still within?" said I to William Scott, who was to be sentry down here till midnight.

He replied that he had not heard a sound. On this I opened the door of the lady's room, and bade Scott hold it open that I might see by the sheen of the cabin lamps. There lay the girl as she had been lying for hours, always breathing with the same regularity, her posture exactly the same. I viewed her attentively, but could not detect that she had moved her head or a limb by as much as the breadth of a finger-nail.

I marveled much as I returned on deck. Was this sleep the forerunner of death? Was life ebbing away as she thus rested? If not, then how long would this slumber last? Yet, thought I, it is best as it is; better that her senses should be thus locked up, than that with eyes brilliant with madness she should be ceaselessly pacing the floor of her room, or with insane cunning watching for an opportunity to steal forth.

I slept during my watch below—that is, from

twelve to four—in the cabin that had been **Don
Lazarillo's,** and Captain Dopping's before him, to
which new quarters I found that Mariana had
brought the charts, chronometer, nautical instruments, and so forth. I slept soundly. Butler
aroused me : all had been well. The breeze had
freshened, he said ; at three o'clock a large line-of-
battle ship had passed within musket-shot ; saving
this, there was nothing to report. I looked in upon
the girl on my way to the deck and found her, as I
was now expecting to find her, in a deep and death-
like sleep.

When the dawn broke I anxiously scanned the
sea line in search of a ship. Every hour of sailing
of this sort was sweeping us closer into the Spanish
coast ; and as I had no intention whatever of re-
linquishing my five seamen until I had got rid of
the two Spaniards, my present keen anxiety was to
heave something into view that would receive them
and carry them off. The rising sun flashed a bright
and joyous morning into the wide scene of heaven
and ocean. The horizon lay clear as the rim of a
lens ; a sweep of delicate blue to either hand of the
glorious wake of the soaring luminary, with the sky
sloping down to it in a dim azure, richly mottled in
the west with clouds ; but there was nothing to be

seen. On this I resolved to shorten sail and to head somewhat more to the southward, where we stood a chance of falling in with the sort of craft we desired to signal. All hands were on deck. I briefly explained my motive, and canvas was forthwith reduced, diminishing the speed of the schooner to within about four miles an hour.

While the men were busy with the ropes, Don Lazarillo's dark and bearded face rose through the main hatch. His eyes swept the horizon, as mine had, and then they settled upon me with a frown of disappointment. His complexion was unwholesome, as from a long night of sleeplessness and anxiety, not to mention the several passions which would contend within him when he reflected on the death of his friend, the complete and tragic failure of the expedition, the prospective loss of his schooner, and the certain loss of the money—doubtless a large sum—with which I was quite sure he had aided Don Christoval in the execution of his scheme to run away with an English heiress. He gave me a sullen bow, pointed with a shrug to the bare ocean, addressed Mariana, whose eyes watched him from the galley-door, and descended into the cabin; but as I happened to be standing close to the companion-way, I was able to observe that he

14

paused, before entering the interior, to make sure that somebody was watching Miss Noble's berth.

He had finished his breakfast by the time I was ready for mine, and as I took my seat he got up and went on deck in silence, casting a single savage glance at the door of the lady's cabin as he walked to the companion-steps. I looked in upon her when I had breakfasted; there was no change in her attitude: her trance, if trance it were, was as profound as ever it had been.

However, as it turned out, Don Lazarillo was not to pass another night aboard La Casandra. And, indeed, seeing what waters we were now navigating, it would have been extraordinary, a thing beyond all average seafaring experience, had hour after hour rolled by without bringing us a sight of a sail. I was eating some dinner, at half-past one o'clock, in the cabin, when Butler put his head into the skylight and called down:

"Mr. Portlack, there's a small vessel standing almost direct for us out of the south'ard and west'ard—bound in, apparently, for the Portugal coast. Shall we signal her?"

"Ay, certainly," cried I. "Heave the schooner to, and run the ensign aloft. I'll be with you presently."

In about ten minutes' time I finished my dinner, swallowed a bumper of the noble Burgundy which had been stowed aft for the consumption of the Spaniards, lighted one of the fine Havana cigars, of which there was a locker half full, and, exchanging a sentence with Trapp, whose turn it was to keep watch on Miss Noble, went on deck. Not above three miles distant, and heading, as it seemed, directly for us, was a square-rigged vessel, a little brig, as she subsequently proved. Her canvas glanced like satin in the sun as she rolled. She was coming leisurely along under all plain sail. There was a color blowing at her main royalmast head, where alone it would have been visible to us, and on seeing it through a glass I made it out to be the Portuguese ensign.

Don Lazarillo was on deck, swathed in his long Spanish cloak, and wearing on his head a large Andalusian hat. He looked like a bandit in an opera. Mariana, whose head was adorned by a long blue cap, shaped like the night-caps men used to sleep in when I was a boy, watched the approaching craft from his favorite skulking-hole, the caboose door.

"She veel do, I hope!" cried Don Lazarillo, on catching sight of me, motioning toward the brig with a theatrical gesture.

"I hope so, indeed," said I, earnestly. "But," cried I, happening to direct my eyes at our gaff end, where flew not the English but the Spanish colors, "what have you got hoisted there, Butler?"

"The only ensign aboard, sir," he answered.

"Upon my word! Yet I might have supposed so. La Casandra is a Spaniard, to all intents and purposes. So much the better," I added, as I sent another glance at the flag we were flying. "The Portuguese may be more willing to oblige the people of that flag's nationality than those whose rag is the red, white, and blue."

The schooner had been hove to, thrown head to wind, her square canvas being furled, and nothing was to be heard but the slopping sound of waters alongside and the straining noises of the fabric as she leaned to the swell, while silently and eagerly we kept our eyes fastened upon the coming Portuguese brig. She drew close to windward, put her helm down, backed her maintop-sail yard, and lay within hailing distance—a prettier model than ever I should have thought to see flying *her* colors, clean in rig, and her canvas fitting her well. The white water raced fountain-like from her bows as she courtesied, ripples of light ran like thrills through her black, wet sides, and there was a frequent leap of white fire from the brass and glass along her quarter-deck.

A tall, gaunt man, whose features were just distinguishable, got upon the rail, and, holding on by a back-stay, pulled off his red cap and hailed us in Portuguese. Don Lazarillo looked round to observe if anybody meant to answer him; then exclaiming, "I understand; I speak his language," he shouted an answer—but an answer that seemed a fathom long; in fact, there was room in Don Lazarillo's response to the Portuguese skipper's hail for the whole story of our adventure. Mariana came and stood alongside the Don. Many cries were exchanged; the gestures were frequent and often frantic. Presently the Portuguese skipper dropped on to his deck, and Don Lazarillo bade Mariana inform me that the man meant to come aboard. In a few minutes the Portuguese brig lowered a boat; her gaunt skipper entered it, accompanied by a couple of men, and pulled the little craft alongside of us.

I had never beheld so strange a figure as that Portuguese skipper. His face was little more than that of a skull, the flesh of which resembled the skin of an old drum where it is darkened by the beating of the sticks; it lay in ridges, as though badly pasted on, and these ridges looked to have become iron-hard through exposure to the weather. His eyes were large, intensely black, and horribly deep sunk, and glowed with what might well have been the fire of fever. Don Lazarillo pronounced some words, haughtily motioning to me; on which the Portuguese skipper gave me such a bow as a skeleton would make, and I pulled off my hat. Then the Spaniard addressed Mariana, who, accosting me in his extraordinary English, said that Don Lazarillo desired to know if it should be left to him to conduct this business of their quitting the schooner. I answered, "Certainly." I had no wish to interfere at all; nor could I be of the slightest use to them, not knowing a syllable of their tongues. On this Don Lazarillo took the Portuguese skipper into the cabin, and with them went the cook.

After a few moments I heard the sound of a cork drawn; this was followed by much animated conversation; but I did not choose to show myself at the skylight under which they were seated, and their accents reached my ear faintly. I said to Butler, with a smile:

"I hope the Don isn't conspiring with the Portugal man to seize the schooner."

"Lord bless ye, Mr. Portlack," he answered

with a grin. "How many of the likes of them chaps in the boat over the side down there would be needed for such a job as that?"

And a grimy, wretched brace of men they were; yellow as mustard, and dark for want of soap, clad in costumes of rags, the lower extremities of which were kept together by being thrust into half-Wellington boots, bronzed with brine.

"Where are you from?" I shouted.

They were squatting in the bottom of the boat like monkeys, and their manner of looking upward was exactly that of monkeys—swift, their gleaming eyes restless, and a queer puckering of their leather lips that seemed a grin. They understood me, and one answered, "Bahia."

"Where are you bound to?"

"Lisbon."

I tried them with one or two more questions, but to no purpose. After the lapse of some twenty minutes Mariana came out of the cabin, and said that Don Lazarillo begged I would be so good as to send two seamen below to convey his effects into the boat.

"Certainly," I answered, and ordered a couple of men to attend upon the Spaniard. Guessing that the Don's effects would be comparatively

trifling, I could not imagine why he required the
services of two men in addition to the cook's help;
until, after a little, first one sailor made his
appearance with his arms full of boxes of cigars,
then the second sailor arrived with a case of wine,
then Mariana came on deck with bags and valises
belonging to the two Dons.   These articles were
handed into the boat, and the seamen and the cook
returned for more.   It was clearly Don Lazarillo's
intention to carry off as much as the Portuguese
boat would hold, and by and by she was lying
alongside deep with wine, cigars, a chest, as I
supposed, of the silver plate, and a variety of other
portable articles.

Don Lazarillo then came up with the Portuguese
captain.   They went to the side and looked over
at the boat, and the Portuguese captain hailed the
men in her, and some unintelligible talk followed.
The boat was then drawn under the gangway by
the two fellows, and without a syllable, but with
one deadly glance of malice at me, Don Lazarillo
entered her.   Mariana, throwing a bundle into her,
followed.   The Portuguese skipper then sprang,
and the boat shoved off.

Fortunately for her inmates, the surface of the
sea flashed and feathered in ripples only, for the

spite or avarice of the Spaniard had so loaded the boat that it needed but a very little weight in the movement of the water to swamp and founder her out of hand.

When her two oars had impelled her a pistol-shot distant from us, Don Lazarillo stood up and proceeded to harangue me in Spanish, with both arms raised and both fists clinched. He rapidly worked himself into a white heat of passion; his voice rose into a penetrating shriek. That he was heaping upon my head every malediction which the language of his country, rich in grotesquely injurious terms, could supply him with, I did not doubt. I picked up a telescope and looked at his face through it, which cool, provoking act so heightened the madness of his wrath that he fell to swaying and toppling about after the manner of a man delirious with drink; whereupon the Portuguese captain, who had sat stolidly looking up at him, to save his own and the lives of the others—for the boat dangerously swayed to the Don's ecstatic gestures—struck him behind in the bend of his legs with the sharp of his hand, and Don Lazarillo vanished in a twinkling in the bottom of the boat. A roar of laughter went up from our men.

" Trim sail, lads, and then heap it on her," I

called out; and, even as the boat lay alongside the brig, with the people in her handing up Don Lazarillo's little cargo, the Casandra, yielding to the impulse of her broad and lofty cloths, was ripping through it to the southward and eastward, the brine spitting at her stem, and the shapely little Portuguese brig veering astern into a Lilliputian toy, her white canvas resembling a hovering butterfly in the confused, misty, and broken fires of the sun's reflection upon the ocean in the south-west.

CHAPTER VIII.

IDA NOBLE.

"Our turn next, sir," exclaimed Butler, coming away from the rail, where he had been standing for a minute looking at the brig under his hand.

"Yes. I shall be sorry to lose you," said I; "but what must be, must be, and you've made up your minds."

"Ay, sir. It is right and proper, indeed, that you should carry the poor lady home; and gladly would we help ye if we durst. But after what's happened——" He violently shook his head. "How far d'ye reckon the coast of Cadiz to be distant, sir?"

"Call it four days at this rate of sailing," said I. Then, looking at him, I continued: "I wish you men would change your minds, and let me set you ashore north of Ushant."

I was proceeding to explain my reason, but he arrested me by an emphatic, "No, sir. Let it be

Cadiz, if you please. The further away the better. All us men have friends at Cadiz, and there are other reasons for our deciding upon that port."

I went below to see what Don Lazarillo had left behind him. The negro lad sat in a chair keeping that watch in the cabin which we continued to maintain spite of the girl's wonderful death-like sleep. It would have been easy, indeed, to have padlocked or in other ways secured the door; but then, if the door had been thus secured, our vigilance would certainly have been relaxed: in which case there was the chance of the cabin being empty at the moment when her consciousness returned, and, consequently, nobody at hand to arrest any dangerous behavior in her.

I found that Don Lazarillo had emptied the locker of its cigars. The negro boy told me that the Spaniard had also carried away the wine which had lain stowed in the lazarette. But there was nothing to grieve me in this news; there were pipes and tobacco on board, and a plentiful stock of cheap wine for the use of the sailors. I entered Don Christoval's cabin and found nothing but the bedding left. The clothes of the dead man had been packed and conveyed to the brig. There was a chest of drawers, and in a corner stood a small table with drawers; these I ransacked, with a faint fancy or hope of meeting with some forgotten letter, some diary or document which Don Lazarillo had neglected to take, and which might throw some fresh light upon this extraordinary expedition. But every drawer was empty.

I was standing lost in thought, with my eyes fixed upon the vacant bunk or sleeping-shelf, musing upon the incidents of the past few days, and wondering into what sort of issue my hand was to shape this adventure, when I was startled by an extraordinary cry, scarcely less alarming in its way than the death-scream that had been uttered by Don Christoval. It was such a cry as a wounded savage might deliver. Before I could reach the door of the berth the negro boy rushed in.

"Oh, massa," he panted, "dah lady's looking out."

My impression was that he had been stabbed. "Are you hurt?" I exclaimed, grasping him by the arm.

"No, sah!"

"Who shrieked just now?"

"I did, sah."

I cuffed him over his woolly head to clear him out of my road, and stepped into the cabin. Miss Noble, with the handle of the cabin door in her grasp, stood looking out with an expression upon her face of such utter bewilderment that but for her costume and my knowing she was the sole occupant of her room, I should not have recognized her. A person watching the motions of a gliding apparition, *knowing* it to be a ghost, beckoning, stalking, compelling, might very well be supposed to stare as that girl did. Her eyes slowly rolled over the interior, as though the organ of vision, stupefied by bewilderment, was scarcely capable of effort. She was deadly pale, yet, spite of the withering influence of her astonishment upon her features, I seemed to find an expression of intelligence in them that most certainly was not to be witnessed before. She breathed swiftly. One side of her hair was now entirely unfastened, and the heavy mass of the dark red tresses lay upon her shoulder and upon her bosom. I instantly looked at her idle hand ; it held nothing.

I surveyed her a little, wondering whether she would speak ; whether reason had been restored to her ; whether there might not happen at any beat of the pulse a sudden horrible transformation in her, a new and blacker exhibition of insanity. Her dark eyes came to mine ; there was an expression of terror in them. She pressed her hand to her forehead, and looked down as though she would sharpen her sight by averting it for a moment from the object at which she gazed, then looked at me again, pleadingly, eagerly, and fearfully.

"Do not you know where you are, Miss Noble?" said I, in the most careless, matter-of-fact manner I could put on.

"I am trying to think," she answered.

"Pray give me your hand," said I.

She extended it as a child might. I led her to an arm-chair and gently obliged her to sit. A decanter half-full of sherry stood in the swing-tray. I poured a little of the wine into a glass, and presented it to her; she took it and drank. Her behavior and looks were absolutely rational, clouded as they were by a bewilderment which her eyes appeared to express as hopeless. She had been fasting for many hours, and I was sure I could not do better than make her take food. I beckoned to Tom, who stood staring at the lady from the other end of the cabin. He approached, though he kept the table between him and Miss Noble. Her bewilderment visibly deepened as her eyes rested on his black face. I directed him to obtain the most delicate refreshments which the cabin larder of the schooner yielded, and to bear a hand.

"You have been long asleep," said I, gently. "You were unconscious when you were brought aboard this vessel—for you know *now* that you are at sea—and you must not wonder that you are bewildered on waking to find yourself in this strange scene."

"Where am I?" she asked, in a voice that was but a little above a whisper, so breathless was she with continued surprise.

"You are on board a schooner called La Casandra. I am acting as her captain. We are now making haste to return to England, to restore you to your home."

"England—home?" she muttered, looking at me, then around her, then down at the dressing-gown she was robed in, then pulling a sleeve of the gown a little way up the arm and gazing at the bracelets upon her wrists. "Why am I here?" she exclaimed, drawing a breath that sounded like a sob.

"Will you not wait till you have eaten a trifle? Nothing has passed your lips for very many hours. As strength returns, your memory will brighten, and I know I shall make you happy by the assurance I am able to give you."

"Why am I here?" she repeated.

I considered it wise to humor her: but to humor her I must tell the truth.

"You are here," said I, "because two Spaniards — one of them named Don Christoval del Padron, and the other styled Don Lazarillo de Tormes—went ashore near your father's estate, on the coast of Cumberland, accompanied by a crew of armed sailors, and forcibly stole you away from your home, carrying you in a state of insensibility to a boat."

She interrupted me at this point by crying out, "Yes, yes, now I remember, now I remember." She clasped her hands and half rose, repeating, "Yes, yes, now I remember," staring past me wildly as she spoke, as though she addressed some one at the other end of the cabin; then burying her face in her hands she sat in silence, rocking herself in the throes of a conflict with memory.

I stood looking on, waiting for nature to have her way with her. The seamen, having got wind of her awakening, had collected at the skylight and were looking down; but fearing that the sight of them might terrify her, I dispersed the group of dark and hairy faces with an angry gesture. Tom arrived with a tray of refreshments. I dispatched him on deck to inform Butler and the others that

15

the lady had returned to consciousness; that her reason had awakened with her, and that she was now as sane as any of us, but that they were to keep quiet and to hold their heads out of view.

Presently the girl looked up; she was weeping, but so silently that I did not know she was crying until I saw her face.

"It has all come back to me," she exclaimed in a broken voice, and shuddering violently. "Did you tell me you were taking me home?"

"Yes, Miss Noble, you are going home."

"Will it be long before we arrive home?"

"Not very long."

"And what has happened to me since I have been here?" said she, looking again down at the rich crimson dressing-gown she was habited in.

"You have been in a sort of stupor," I answered, "but you have awakened strong and well; or let me say, in a very little while you will be strong and well. But you must eat, if you please, and while you eat you shall ask any questions you like, and I will answer you."

I put the plate beside her, and noticed with gladness that she eyed it somewhat wistfully. Indeed, if anybody were ever nearly starved, she was; though medical men to whom I have stated her case have since told me that persons visited with these extraordinary fits of slumber can live for days, and even for weeks, without food.

Tom had been careful not to put a knife on the tray; but there was a fork, and with it I placed a thin slice of ham between two white biscuits and presented this sea-sandwich to her, and she began to eat. She ate the whole of it, and then I made her another and gave her a little more sherry, and now I could observe how excellently this refresh ment served her as medicine; for every moment seemed to diminish something of her bewilderment, while intelligence brightened in her eyes, and a very faint bloom from the improved action of her heart sifted into her complexion

Suddenly, with a start, and with a wild and terrified look around the cabin, she asked me where the two Spaniards were. The idea of them, borne on the current of the thoughts and fancies flowing through her brain, had, as I might judge, but that instant entered her consciousness. Now it was not to be supposed that I could tell her she had with her own hand slain one of those Spaniards; and no purpose, therefore, could be served by informing her that one of them was dead.

"They have left the vessel," I answered.

"Will they return?" she cried.

"No, indeed; I will take care of that. You
need not fear that they will trouble you any more."

Her countenance relaxed its expression of terror, and her eyes met mine with a soft and touching
look of gratitude in them. She then sighed deeply,
and pressed her hand to her forehead.

"Pray, Miss Noble, tell me how you feel?"
said I.

"My head swims," she answered. "The motion
of this vessel affects me."

Now that might well have been so, strange as it
may seem. She would suffer from sea-sickness
neither in her trance nor in her madness; but now
that both were passed, now that her real nature was
re-established in her, she must needs begin to suffer
as she would have suffered from this same sea-sickness at the beginning of the voyage had she been
brought on board in her senses. It seemed to me a
most wholesome, reassuring sign, though I would
not say so, for I desired to preserve her from all
suspicion of the hideous state she had passed
through.

"Suppose," said I, "that you lie down and endeavor to obtain some sleep. What you have awakened from was stupor, and there can be no refresh-

ment in stupor. A few hours of wholesome, natural rest are sure to work wonders."

She rose in silence, but with consent in her eyes. Observing that her movements were unsteady, I gently held her arm and directed her steps to her berth. She got into her bunk, and I paused to inquire if there was anything I could do for her.

"Nothing," she answered in a low voice. "I am grateful for your kindness. Everything has come back to me. Oh, yes, I now remember that dreadful night—that dreadful night! But you are not deceiving me?"

"In what?"

"You tell me that Don Christoval and his friend are not in this vessel."

"Rest your poor heart, Madame. I swear to you as an English seaman that they are out of this vessel, and that you will never be troubled by them again."

"Where are they?" she asked.

"We will talk about them by and by."

She closed her eyes, and I stood beside her a few minutes, then went out, calling to Tom to come and keep watch, with a threat to rope's-end him if he shrieked again should the lady suddenly show herself, for that she was now as sane as he or I was.

I went on deck heartily rejoiced by this restoration of the poor lady's mind. It cleared me of a heavy load of anxiety. Now I could contemplate taking charge of the schooner with only Tom to help me until I could procure further assistance: this I could think of without half the misgiving which before worked in me when my mind went to it. On my showing myself, Butler, who was in charge, immediately approached me.

"I see the poor lady's woke up at last, sir."

"Yes," said I.

"And Tom says she has her intellect sound again."

"It is true, and thank God for it," said I.

"Strange, Mr. Portlack," said he, after biting for a moment or two meditatively on the piece of tobacco in his cheek, "that the poor lady should come to just at the time that there Spaniard goes off, as one might say. There's a tarm to fit the likes of such a traverse, but I forgets it."

"A coincidence," said I.

"Well, that'll do, I dessay, though there's another word a-running in my head. And how do the lady relish the notion of having stuck the big Span-iard?"

"Now listen to me, Butler," said I, "and repeat

what I am about to tell to your mates in the most powerful voice you can command, and in the strongest words you can employ. Under no circumstances whatever, on no consideration whatever, must the lady be given to know that she committed that act. Tell her of it, and in all probability you will drive her mad for good and all."

"There's no fear of any of us ever a-telling her of it," he replied, with a sort of sulky astonishment working in his face at the energy with which I had addressed him; "but she'll have to hear of it some of these days, won't she, sir?"

"Not from us," said I, "and therefore what is going to happen some of these days will be no business of ours."

"That's true enough," said he.

"There is another point that may be worth our consideration. Briefly, the lady has now her senses; she has a clear eye, and may very likely prove to have a keen memory. I will take care that your names are not known to her; and should she ever come on deck while you remain on board, I would advise you and your mates to show as little of yourselves as the navigation of the ship will suffer."

He looked thoughtful, and fell to stroking his

chin. "Yes, by thunder! Mr. Portlack, you're right," he exclaimed. "If she gets to hear our names, and is able to describe us, why! Tell ye what it is, sir : the sooner we five men are off, the better ; and until we've cleared out, I hope you won't encourage her to come on deck too often."

Having tasted no food for some hours, I went below, and dispatched Tom to procure me some supper. While he waited upon me the following conversation took place between us :

"You must never at any time, or on any occasion, say, either aboard this schooner or ashore, that the lady in the cabin yonder killed the Spaniard."

"No, sah."

"If you do, you and I, who are to convey this lady home, will be charged as accomplices in the awful crime of bloody murder."

"I'll be berry car'fu', sir."

"A single hint from you might lead to you and me being hanged by the neck until we are dead. On the other hand, if you keep silent, I will take care that you are rewarded ; and if you have had enough of the sea, I dare say the friends of the lady will find you some comfortable berth ashore."

The lad's black face was somewhat complicated by expression. There was mingled fright and delight in his wide grin and the stare of his large, bland, dusky African eyes.

"Mind!" said I.

And here let me own that my desire that the murder of the Spaniard should be kept a profound secret was largely—indeed almost wholly—a selfish one. For, first, I never doubted that, if the girl came to hear of what she had done, the thought of it working in a brain still weak with recent craziness would render her incurably mad, and so immeasurably increase my present anxieties and the trouble I should be put to to carry her home. Next, I wished the dreadful deed kept secret, since this singular expedition having caused me trouble and grief enough already upon the high seas, I was by no means anxious that darker worries should grow out of it on my arrival on shore.

I saw nothing of the lady that evening, nor, indeed, throughout the night. Two or three times I knocked upon her door to inquire if she needed anything, and once only she answered. Her reply satisfied me that her mind was hers again; that, in short, there had been no relapse since I had left her. However, to provide against all risk, I arranged that the seamen should keep a look-out in the cabin as heretofore.

I had charge of the deck from four till eight. It blew continually a fine breeze of wind, and hour after hour the schooner swept through it as though driven by powerful engines. I guessed, if the vessel maintained her present rate of sailing, that the men would be enabled to leave me before forty-eight hours had passed. Daybreak showed us several ships on the sea line. They were all of them small vessels, and standing, with the exception of one, to the north. The man Scott, who was at the helm, said that it was a pity his mates could not see their way to transshipping themselves aboard a craft, instead of making for Cadiz in the cutter.

"Why don't you stop with me?" said I.

"No, no!" he exclaimed.

"But listen. Could not we three—you, me, and the negro boy—carry the schooner into Penzance, say, where you might go ashore at once, take the coach for London, and vanish much more entirely than ever you will by going to Cadiz?"

"No, sir, no; there's to be no going home with me. I should be a fool to trust myself in England. I'm too respectable a man to live in any country where I'm ' wanted.' "

"Well, then," said I, "Butler's scheme of the cutter and of Cadiz is the practicable one, and you must adopt it. You talk of my transshipping you. What story am I to tell the captain whom I ask to receive you? You don't look like mutineers, and not one of you is clever enough to act such a part as would enable me to spin my yarn without exciting suspicion. Now, suspicion is the last thing we wish to excite."

" True, sir," said Scott.

It was about a quarter before eight when the negro boy, who had been preparing the table for my breakfast, came on deck to tell me that the lady was in the cabin. I looked through the skylight and beheld her sitting in an arm-chair. She saw me, and bowed with a slight smile. I lifted the lid of the skylight that I might converse with her, and called down, " Good morning, Miss Noble. I hope you are feeling very much better?"

" I am very much better, thank you," she answered, in a voice soft indeed, but whose tone and firmness were ample warrant of returning strength.

" I hope to join you shortly. My watch on deck expires in a few minutes. It is a fine bright morning and there is a noble sailing breeze, and the schooner is going through the water like a witch."

" I should like to go on deck," she said, " but I have no covering for my head."

I recommended her to wait till after breakfast, when we would go to work to see what the schooner could yield her in the shape of head-gear; and shortly afterward, on Butler arriving to relieve me, I joined her. She had dressed her hair, and this and the effect of the comfortable night she had passed had made another being of her. With her recovery, or, at all events, with her improvement, had reappeared what I might suppose her habitual nature. Her countenance expressed decision of character; her gaze was gentle but steadfast; and in the set of her lips there was such a suggestion of self-control as even my untutored sea-faring eye could not miss. I now took notice, too, of her well-bred air. In the hurry and agitation of the preceding day I had missed this quality, or she may have failed to express it. But now, on my entering the cabin, and on her rising and extending her hand, I was instantly sensible of the presence of the high-born lady.

Almost in the first words she pronounced she asked me for my name. I gave it to her, and with mingled dignity and sweetness she thanked me for my sympathy and attention. Our discourse was chiefly about her health, the sort of night she had passed, and the like, while Tom was putting the breakfast upon the table. We then seated ourselves.

She ate with appetite, but was so reserved at first that I thought to myself, " Now, Madame, I suppose you intend I shall thoroughly understand you are a lady of high degree, between whom and a second mate in the merchant service there stretches a so- cial interval wide as the Atlantic Ocean ; and though I had hoped you would tell me your story and help me to a clear understanding of Don Chris- toval and his expedition, you mean to disappoint me through your new resolution to assert your dignity."

But never was I more mistaken in a lady's character. I could see her glancing from time to time at the negro boy, who lost no opportunity of staring at her in return, as though he expected to see her at any moment snatch up a knife. I be- lieved I could read her thoughts, and told the boy to go on deck and stop there till I called him. She trifled for a bit with her rings ; then, with a little show of nervousness, though her accents did not falter, she said to me :

" Mr. Portlack, from the moment of my fainting on that dreadful night, down to my awaking yes- terday, I seem to remember nothing. I say I *seem*, and yet I am haunted by a sort of horrid memory— how shall I express it ? It is the shadow of a recol-

lection, and that recollection again is, as it were,"
pressing her brow as though struggling to deeply
realize her thought, " no more than the memory
of the shadow of something horrible. Am I meaningless to you ? "

"No."

She viewed me anxiously and searchingly, and
said, " Have I been mad ? "

" You were insensible when you were brought
aboard, and you awoke from your extraordinary
stupor for the first time yesterday."

" Mr. Portlack, tell me, have I been out of my
mind ? "

Hating a lie as I do, I was yet resolved that she
should not know the truth, and I said "No" with
so much emphasis that her face instantly cleared.
She smiled, and clasped her hands. " Ah ! " she
exclaimed, breathing deep as though she sighed,
" in so long and dreadful a slumber I must have
dreamed many fearful dreams."

I wished to disengage her mind from this subject, and I was also desirous that she should understand, without further loss of time, how it happened
that I made one of the kidnaping gang.

" With your permission," said I, " I will tell
you my story, which, I believe, you will think a

strange one even in the experiences of a sea-faring person."

She watched me with attention, and I proceeded to relate my adventures, beginning with the Ocean Ranger, and then going on to the American ship, to my distressful and perilous situation in the open boat, and then to this schooner La Casandra falling in with me; thus I steadily worked my way right through my own yarn, omitting nothing save the incident of the death of Don Christoval. That she was a young lady of much strength of character I might now be sure of by her manner of listening to me. I was graphic enough, particularly in my description of our arrival off the coast of Cumberland; nevertheless, she attended to me with composure, with firm lips and steady regard. No exclamation escaped her. Once or twice she sighed, and once she colored, as though from some sudden passion of resentment swiftly controlled.

"And now, Miss Noble," said I, "I hope I have made you understand how it happens that I am here?"

"Perfectly," she answered, "and I am glad that you *are* here, Mr. Portlack. But you have not told me what has become of Don Christoval and his friend."

There was nothing for it—I must tell another falsehood; but Heaven would forgive me, for I meant well. So I answered that I had informed them, on learning that she was not Madame del Padron, that it was my intention to carry her home, and that on my arrival my first business would be to inform against them for having abducted **her**; whereupon they had prayed to be transshipped to a passing vessel; to which, after reflection, I consented, and the two scoundrels were transferred to a little Portuguese brig on the preceding day.

She sank into thought. After a while she lifted up her head and gazed slowly and with curiosity round her at the pictures, the mirrors, and the other furniture in the cabin. Her eyes next went to her bracelets, and they then met mine. I waited for her to speak.

"How long is it now, Mr. Portlack, since I was stolen from my father's house?"

"This is the sixth day of your absence."

"What will my father and mother think? They can not have been able to *do* anything. That will be the hardest part to my father. They will have no idea into what part of the world I was to be carried. Will they even know that this vessel was lying off the coast to receive me?"

"Oh, yes," said I, "they will know that. Some one is certain to have followed the sailors and the Spaniards as they marched with you to the boat."

"Would there be any papers, any letters, do you think," said she, "on the body of the man who you said was killed, from which my father might learn that this vessel's destination was Cuba?"

"I do not know. Most probably not."

"What a wanton act of wickedness! What unnecessary, barbarous cruelty!" she exclaimed. "Had I been driven mad, it would not have been strange. We had just arrived from a ball, when my father cried out that there was a crowd of men outside. He told me to run upstairs. I can not imagine that he suspected the errand on which they had come. I believed that the men had arrived to plunder the house: it is situated on a lonely part of the coast. I went into a room, and almost at that moment I heard the report of a gun. The house is an old-fashioned building, the walls very thick. I was so far away from the hall that no sound reached me, but in a short time I heard footsteps, and the noise of doors violently opened, and the voices of men exclaiming in Spanish. The door of my room was tried; I had turned the key, but the lock was an old one. The two Spaniards

16

put their shoulders against the door, and it flew open; then I recollect a few moments of struggling and shrieking, and nothing more."

" Did you never fear that Don Christoval would one day or night attempt to carry you off?"

" Never," she responded, with a note of vehemence disturbing her calm tones, and I saw a flash in her brown eyes.

" He evidently kept himself acquainted with your movements."

" Yes," she answered; " in another week we were going abroad. We should have been starting about now, or to-morrow."

" He told me that. Who was the spy he employed, I wonder?"

She reflected, and answered: " No member of our household, I am sure. What sort of person is Don Lazarillo de Tormes?"

I described him, and perceived by her way of listening that she had never seen him, and indeed had never heard of him.

" You may take it, Miss Noble," said I, " that whoever Don Lazarillo may have been, he found the money for this adventure."

" That must have been so," she answered; " Don Christoval is poor."

"Had he any property in Cuba?"

"I believe not," she answered.

"Forgive me for being inquisitive. Was—I mean, is the man in any way related to you?"

"He is. He is a distant connection on my father's side. His father was a Spaniard, and, I have always understood, of noble blood. Don Christoval was in England, and called upon us when we were in London. We afterward met him in Paris. My father disliked him, and it came to his forbidding him from holding any communication with us. He then challenged my brother to a duel, and, unknown to my father and mother, my brother attended with a friend, a lieutenant in the Royal Navy; but Don Christoval did not appear. That is entirely all that I can tell you about the man, Mr. Portlack."

"I felt," said I, "that he was lying when he spoke of you as his wife. But how was it possible to make sure of the truth, one way or the other? He put his story so persuasively, his voice was so sweet, he was so very handsome, that any one believing in his tale could not but have pitied him, even to the degree of feeling willing to help him to recover what he called his own."

She slightly colored, and said, "He only wanted my money."

Here I might have complimented her, but I was an off-hand sailor, without any talent for drawing-room civilities.

I need not dwell at length upon what passed between Miss Noble and me on this our first opportunity for enjoying a long chat. It was natural that we should again and again travel over the same ground. Though she did not repeat her question whether she had been out of her mind, I noticed, in her references to her state of catalepsy or stupor, a haunting uneasiness, as though the shadow of some black dream lay upon her in tormenting shapelessness and illusiveness. I can fancy that it resembled one of those ideas which visit most of us in our lifetime—the idea that we have felt, suffered, or done something in another sphere of being.

She was clearly a lady of strong constitution. She showed no traces of the condition she had been in for nearly a week. One would have thought to see her haggard, bloodless, famine-pinched, with pale lips and unlighted eyes ; but, making due allowance for the costume of crimson dressing-gown and for the absence of divers finishing details of toilet, I could not conceive that she, at any time in her life, could have looked much better than she now did. May be her profound sleep had cleansed her

countenance of the dreadful marks which the talons
of the fiend Madness commonly grave upon the
human face. Be this as it may, her health seemed
excellent as I sat conversing with her at that break-
fast-table; her calm voice had the true music of
good breeding; her remarks exhibited no common
order of perception and good sense, and to my mind
—though it is said that sailors are easy to please—
she needed no other face than her own, with its soft
brown eyes, and purely feminine lineaments, and
dark red hair, massive, abundant, and glowing, to
be as fascinating a lady as a man could hope to meet
with in English or any other society.

I had, in the course of our conversation, told her
very honestly what the sailors intended to do. I
added that they were right in endeavoring to escape
from the consequences of a wrong into the perpe-
tration of which they had been basely betrayed by
the lies of Don Christoval and his friend. I had
then explained that I should be left alone in the
schooner with the negro boy, but that I had not the
least doubt of promptly obtaining all the help I
needed to carry the vessel safely and comfortably
home. This made her ask how long it might take
us to reach home.

"Eight or ten days," I answered.

"What, meanwhile, am I to do for clothes?" said she; and, with something of unconsciousness in her manner, as though her fingers were governed by a thought in her head, she opened her dressing-gown and revealed herself in ball attire.

Though she had been thus appareled for a week there seemed to be nothing soiled, nothing faded, in this aspect of her. It was the suddenness of the revelation, I dare say, that gave to her form the brilliance I found in it. Then, there was also the contrast of the rich crimson dressing-gown to heighten this instant splendor of attire and the incomparable whiteness of her neck and shoulders, though these were still defaced by several long, ugly black scratches. She buttoned the dressing-gown to her throat again, and said, with a smile full of self-possession, but sweetened by a little expression of sadness :

"This is not the kind of dress that one would wear at sea, Mr. Portlack."

"It is very beautiful," said I in my simple way.

"The skirt is badly torn," she exclaimed. "Those wretches must have treated me very roughly, even after I had fainted."

"You certainly will require warmer clothing than that ball-dress," said I. "Stay! an idea occurs to me. Was it Don Christoval—yes, I believe it was Don Christoval, who informed me—who implied rather—that he had made some provisions for you in the matter of dress." I shouted through the skylight for Tom. The boy arrived. "Go and ask Mr. Butler," said I, "if he can tell me in what part of the vessel Captain Dopping stowed the wearing apparel which was taken on board by Don Christoval for the use of this lady."

The boy went on deck. Presently Butler's head showed in the skylight. There was a shawl round his throat, that covered his mouth to the height of his nostrils, and he wore a sou'-wester, the forward thatch of which he had turned down, while the earlappets hid his cheeks. It was clear he did not intend that Miss Noble should see more of his face than might serve him to breathe with.

"Beg pardon, sir," he said in a muffled hurricane note, talking through his shawl. "Here's this here Tom come with some message from you, and I don't know what he means." I explained. "Ho! yes," said he; "I understand now. There's a chest of garments, I believe, stowed away down in the lazareet."

In less than twenty minutes the negro lad and I had explored the lazarette, discovered the chest,

lugged it into Miss Noble's cabin, and there left it
open.   All that it contained I could not tell you,
but when I next saw Miss Noble she was wearing
a green dress of some light, good material, the waist
of which was secured by a band, and on her head
was a plain straw hat of a sort to prove very serv-
iceable to a lady at sea.

CHAPTER IX.

Now, until we had closed the Spanish coast, that
is to say, during the following four days, nothing
happened of such moment as deserves your attention. The men kept themselves as much as possible
out of sight of Miss Noble, and every fellow whose
turn it was to stand at the helm invariably arrived so concealed about the face that I would often
find it difficult to give him his right name. The
sailors' dread of being observed by Miss Noble grew
speedily into a real inconvenience; it came, indeed,
very near to hindering me, in the daytime when the
lady was on deck, from navigating the schooner;
and to end it I took occasion, when we sat below at
some meal or other, to tell her of what the men
were afraid; with the result, that until the fellows
left us her visits to the deck were very few, and
chiefly in the dusk.

It was four days from the date of the transshipment of Don Lazarillo and the cook that by my computation we arrived within ten leagues of the coast of Spain, the port of Cadiz bearing about east-by-south. It was a sunny morning, with a pleasant breeze. We hove the schooner to, for I did not think proper to approach the land nearer than thirty miles. Here and there was a gleam of white canvas upon the horizon; and I thought to myself, reflecting in the interests of the men, their departure must not be witnessed, nor must anything be near enough to fall in with them and to have the schooner in sight also; therefore I hove La Casandra to at a distance of about ten leagues from the port of Cadiz, nothing being visible but one or two sail, hull down.

Everything was in readiness. You will believe that the boat, owing to the men's anxiety to get away, had been long before this morning provisioned and equipped. She was launched through the gangway just as she had been launched off the Cumberland coast on that silent, tragic night; then, while she lay alongside, the seamen, in obedience to my command, went to work to reduce sail upon the schooner, so that there would be little left for me and Tom to do should it come on to blow before we could procure help. While this was doing

Miss Noble remained in the cabin. Everything being ready, Butler stepped up to me with his hand extended. I grasped and shook it.

"Good-by, sir, and we all hope, I'm sure, that you'll have a safe and happy run home."

"Good-by, Butler — good-by, my lads. You have behaved very well. I thank you for the willingness with which you have done your work under me. See that the yarn you have in your heads you all stick to, so that you'll be able to speak as with one tongue when you get ashore."

"Trust us, sir," said Scott.

"I hope the lady thoroughly understands," said Trapp, "how it happened that we five Englishmen was led into a job which ne'er a man of us would have touched, no, not for five times the money received, had the true meaning of it been explained?"

"She does. And now you had better be off."

They entered the boat, stepped the mast, and I gave Butler the course to steer by the little box compass that had been placed in the stern-sheets. They then hoisted the sail, and as the boat slid away from the shadow of the schooner's side, they all stood up and loudly cheered me. I halloed a cheer back to them with a flourish of my cap, then stepped aft, and, putting the helm **over**, brought the schooner with her head to west-north-west.

"Come and lay hold of the tiller, Tom." The negro boy arrived. "Miss Noble," said I, putting my head into the companion-way, "the men have left the schooner."

She at once came on deck, and stood looking in silence at the cutter as she swept swiftly eastward under the white square of her lug.

"We are lonely indeed, now," she presently exclaimed, bringing her eyes from the boat to cast them round the horizon.

"Yes," said I, "but we are going home," and I pointed to the compass.

But she was right, for all that. Lonely the schooner looked with her deserted decks and small canvas, and lonely I felt, not so much at the beginning as later on, when the rolling hours brought the night along, without heaving anything into view that we could turn to account. Miss Noble earnestly wished to help; she assured me she could steer; she was sprung, she said, from a naval stock, and she told me that salt water had run in the veins of several generations on her father's side, and that she was to be trusted at the helm. And, indeed, I found that she steered perfectly well; she held the

yacht's head steady to her course; and as half the
art of steering lies in that, the most experienced
man could not have done more.

Her taking the helm enabled the boy to cook
for us, and it gave me an opportunity to obtain
sights, to attend to the sails, and the like. Yet,
when day broke next morning, I well remember
heartily praying that I should not have to pass, sin-
gle-handed, such another night as we had managed
to scrape through. I was on deck all night long.
I obliged Miss Noble to go below and take some
rest, and Tom slept at my feet while I grasped the
tiller, ready to relieve me when I was exhausted
with standing. Happily it was a fine night; a
warm wind blew out of the west, and the stars
shone purely with a few shadows of clouds sailing
down the eastern slope.

It was shortly after eight o'clock, while I stood
near the tiller drinking a cup of chocolate which
Tom had brought me out of the galley, where
he had lighted a fire, that, happening to look
astern, I spied a sail. Nothing else was in sight,
and I had but to look once to know that she was
overtaking us. This, indeed, must have been practicable to the clumsiest wagon afloat; for the canvas the schooner was under, merry as was the breeze

that whipped the sea into snow and fire under the risen sun, was scarcely sufficient to drive her along at four miles in the hour.

When I had drunk my chocolate I bade Tom prepare some breakfast for Miss Noble, who was, or had been, resting on a sofa in the cabin. When the girl had finished her meal she came on deck. And now the overtaking vessel had risen to her hull, and in the telescope which I pointed at her was proving herself a large ship, with a black and white band and a red gleam of copper under the checkered side as she leaned from the breeze.

"I wish she may not be an English frigate," said I to Miss Noble.

"Why?" she asked.

"Because," said I, "she is sure to prove too inquisitive to be convenient. She'll be sending a lieutenant on board; he will see you; he will ask questions; he will demand the schooner's papers; he will not be satisfied, and will return to his ship for instructions; and we want to get home comfortably, Miss Noble."

"I understand you," she answered. "But an English frigate! What security, what safety is there in the very sound of the words!"

I waited a little while, and then, again leveling

the glass at the vessel, I clearly perceived that she was not an English frigate, but a large merchant-man, resembling a man-of-war in many details, saving the row of grinning artillery, the white line of hammocks, the heavy tops, and a peculiar cut of canvas that could never be mistaken by a nautical eye in those days of tacks and sheets. Apparently she was a troop ship out of the Mediterranean; there were many red spots of uniform upon her forecastle past the yawn and curves of the white and swelling jibs. And, indeed, she had need to be a hired transport, for nothing of her rig would have any business in the Mediterranean, and nothing homeward bound from the Indies or the Australias was likely to be met with so far to the eastward as was the longitude of the waters we were in. I hoisted the Spanish ensign, and left it flying at half-mast.

"Now, Miss Noble," said I, "what story shall I tell those people, should they heave to and send a boat, as I hope and believe they will?"

She gazed at me inquiringly.

"If I give them the whole truth," said I, "it will run like wildfire throughout the ship. The vessel will probably arrive before we do; there are crowds of people on board to talk; the news of the outrage done you and yours will be circulated, printed; it will become everybody's gossip. Now, would Captain Noble wish this? Would my lady, your mother, desire this?"

"No, they would not," she answered, after a pause. "You are kind and wise to ask the question. The thought did not occur to me when I wished that yonder vessel might prove an English frigate."

"Then I must invent a story," said I.

"But did not you say," she asked, "that when we arrived at an English port you would be obliged to hand the schooner over to the authorities of the port, to whom you would relate the truth, as it would be impossible and most unwise to attempt to deceive them? Those were your words, Mr. Portlack."

"Yes, I remember; those were my words. Well, Miss Noble?"

"Well," said she, "don't you see that, since you must tell the truth when you arrive in England, this wretched story will have to be made public in any case?"

"No," said I, "there is a difference. Yonder is a ship full of soldiers and sailors, and others—gossips all, no doubt. To give them the truth—and to give it to the captain or the mate is to give it to them all —is tantamount to publishing your story throughout

England, whether you will or not; but to communicate with the receiver of wrecks is another matter.
There is official reserve to depend upon. Your father, too, will not be wanting in influence. To me,
Miss Noble, it is all one. I desire to be influenced
by your wishes."

"My wish certainly is," said she in her calm,
emphatic way of speaking, "that as little as possible
of what has befallen me should be known."

"Then," said I, "I will ask you to step into the
cabin and keep in your own berth out of sight until
the visit I hope to receive is ended."

She went below forthwith.

Half an hour later the large full-rigged hired
transport Talavera had ranged alongside La Casandra, easily within ear-shot. She was crowded with
troops; numbers of military officers in undress uniform surveyed us from the poop. A tall man in
a frock coat and a cap with a naval peak stood
upon a hen-coop, and hailed to know what was the
matter.

"My men have deserted," I cried back; "there
are but this negro boy and myself to carry the
schooner to an English port. Can you lend me a
couple of hands?"

"I will send a boat," he exclaimed, very easily

17

perceiving that it was impossible for me to board him.

A boat in charge of a mottled-faced, jolly-looking, round-shouldered man, about thirty years of age, swept alongside, and the jolly-looking man came on board.

"Are you the master?" said he.

"Yes," said I.

"Short of men, hey?" said he. "So I should suppose, if *he's* your crew, "bursting into a laugh as he indicated the negro boy with a motion of his chin. "How come you to be at sea with no more crew than one little nigger?"

"My crew," said I, "were composed of five English sailors. They were shipped at Cadiz. Yesterday they took the boat, and sailed away to the coast of Spain in her, saying *they* weren't going to England. Can you lend me a couple of hands?"

"What's the name of this craft?" said he, looking up at the Spanish ensign.

"La Casandra."

"From Cadiz, d'ye say?—to where?"

"To Penzance," said I, naming the first port that entered my head.

"Who's the owner?"

"Don Lazarillo de Tormes."

He asked several further questions of a like sort, and seemed perfectly satisfied with my answers. I invited him to step below and drink a glass of wine, but he declined, saying that his ship was in too great a hurry to get home to allow him to stop and take a friendly glass on the road.

He had not long returned to the Talavera when the boat, in charge of a midshipman, came alongside the schooner again, and a couple of young sailors, each with a sailor's bag upon his shoulder, climbed over the side. The midshipman, looking up, called out to me: "They're a couple of Dutchmen, but the captain guesses they'll serve your turn." I told him to give my hearty thanks to the captain for his kindness. He then went back to his ship, which immediately swung her yards, and in a little while a wide space of water separated the two vessels.

"Dutchman" is a generic word employed by sailors to designate Germans, Swedes, Danes, and others of the northern nationalities. These two Dutchmen proved to be, the one a young Swede, who spoke English very imperfectly, and the other a young Dane, whose knowledge of English was almost wholly restricted to the names of ropes and sails; both of them smart, respectful young fellows, without curiosity, accepting their sudden change of life with the proverbial indifference of the sailor.

I had intended, for the convenience of Miss Noble, to carry the schooner to Whitehaven ; but before
we gained the parallel of Land's End it came on to
blow heavily from the north and west—so heavily,
and with such an ugly, menacing look of continu-
ance in the wide, dark, greenish scowl of the sky,
that I thought proper to shift my helm for the
English Channel. *There* we encountered terrible
weather. I hoped to make some near port, but,
owing to the thickness and to the gale that had
veered due west, I could do nothing but keep the
schooner running until we were off the South Fore-
land. The weather then moderating, I steered for
Ramsgate harbor, and the schooner was safely
moored alongside the wall of the East Pier in six
days to the hour from the date of our receiving the
two seamen from the Talavera.

You will suppose that Miss Noble long before
this had written a letter—nay, had written four
letters—to her father ready for instantly posting on
her arrival anywhere. It seems that he had four
addresses—his house in Cumberland, his house in
town, and two clubs, one in London and one in the
north—and she was determined that her letters

should not be delayed through his absence from
one address or another. These letters were immediately posted, but communication in those days
was not as it is now, and if it happened that her
father was in Cumberland, then, let him post it
and coach it as he would, it must occupy him hard
upon four days—and perhaps five days—to reach
Ramsgate.

Certain Custom House officers came on board
and rummaged the schooner for contraband cargo.
They stared hard at the cabin furniture, and moved
and groped here and there with eyes full of suspicion. I told Miss Noble that my immediate business now lay at the Custom House, and I begged to
know what her plans were, that I might help her to
further them.

"I will go to a hotel," she answered, "and there
wait for my father. As you are going into the
town, will you engage a sitting-room and bedroom
for me at the best hotel in the place? And I will
also ask you to order a trunk-maker to send a portmanteau down to this schooner, otherwise I shall not
know how to pack my ball-dress and jewelry. This
dress," said she, looking down at the robe in which
she was attired, and which had formed a portion of
the apparel that Don Christoval had laid in for her,

" I shall continue to wear until my father brings me the dresses I have written for."

" I will do what you ask," said I, and, leaving her on board, I climbed the ladder affixed to the pier wall, and bent my steps in the direction of the Custom House.

The receiver was a little, eager-looking man, afflicted with several nervous disorders. He could neither sit nor stand for any length of time; he blinked hideously, and he also stuttered. My tale took the form of a deposition, and I omitted no single point of it, save the assassination of Don Christoval.

" This," said the little receiver, stammering and blinking—" this," he exclaimed, when I had come to an end, " is a very extraordinary story, sir."

" It is," said I.

" Captain Noble is a well-known gentleman," said he. " I was for a short time on duty at Whitehaven, and heard much of him."

" His daughter has written to him," said I, " and he will doubtless be here as fast as he can travel. And what about the schooner ? "

" I must wait for instructions," he answered ; "your deposition will be sent to head-quarters."

" Have I not a lien upon her ? "

"For what?" said he.

"For services rendered."

"Seems the other way about, don't it?" said he, with his stammer. "The services appear to have been rendered by her to you."

"There are two men and a boy who want their wages," said I.

"Who is the owner, d'ye say?" exclaimed the little man.

"Don Lazarillo de Tormes."

"Well, he will be communicated with."

"No, he won't, though," said I. "We shall never hear anything more of Don Lazarillo de Tormes. What! do you think that the man would dare come forward and claim his schooner on top of an outrage which would earn him transportation for life, could they get hold of him in this country?"

"If he doesn't come forward," said the little receiver, blinking at me, "and if the schooner re-remains unclaimed for any length of time, why, then she will be sold; and there'll be your opportunity for asserting your rights."

I walked into the town, leaving the little receiver putting on his hat to view the wonderful schooner, with a hope, too, of catching a sight of

Miss Noble. I obtained the required accommodation for the lady at the Albion Hotel; then, observing a shop in which some trunks were displayed, I told the shopkeeper to send one of them, or a portmanteau if he had such a thing, down to the schooner La Casandra. Entering the street again, I walked a little way, and, finding myself in the market-place, stopped to consider. I did not possess a farthing of money in my pocket, and it would take me some time to draw my little savings out of that London bank in which they were deposited; but money for immediate needs I must have, and, addressing a porter in a white apron, who stood in the market-place smoking a pipe, I asked him to direct me to a pawnbroker. He pointed with his pipe up the street, and proceeding in that direction I presently observed the familiar sign of the three balls. I entered, and put down the gold chain and watch that had belonged to Don Christoval, and for it I received twenty sovereigns and a ticket.

I then returned to the schooner, where I found Miss Noble in the cabin reasoning with the trunk-maker, who had arrived, bearing with him two or three samples of the desired goods.

"He will not trust me, Mr. Portlack! and yet

it is true—and too absurd—that I can make him nothing but promises of payment."

"Pray, how much do you want?" said I.

"Fourteen shillings," she answered, and she added tranquilly, with a slight smile, "To think that I should want fourteen shillings!"

I put down a sovereign; the man gave me change, shouldered the remaining boxes, and went away.

Having escorted Miss Noble to her hotel, I again returned to the schooner, which I intended should be my home until after the arrival of Captain Noble. The two sailors asked me what they should do. I advised them to ship aboard a collier and make their way to London, where they would easily find some one to advise them as to what proceedings they should take in respect of reward for the assistance they had rendered me in carrying the schooner home. Next day they found a collier wanting men, and, giving them a sovereign, I bade them farewell. I never heard of them again.

Meanwhile, I kept the negro boy on board the schooner.

We had arrived at Ramsgate on a Wednesday morning. On the afternoon of the following Tuesday I was pacing the deck of the schooner as she lay moored against the pier wall. The harbor master had not long left me. An hour we had spent together, I in talking and he in listening; for the receiver, with whom he was intimate, had dropped many hints of my story to him over a glass of whisky and water one night, and he told me he could not rest until he had heard my version of the extraordinary romance. It was a brilliant afternoon; a fresh breeze from the west swept into the harbor between the pier-heads, and the water danced in light. A few smacks, bowed down by their weight of red canvas, were endeavoring to beat out to sea. A number of wherries straining at their painters frolicked in the flashful tumble, past which was the slope of beach with galleys and small boats high and dry, and many forms of lounging boatmen. On the milk-white heights of chalk the windows of the houses glanced in silver fires, which came and went in a sort of breathing way as they blazed out and were then extinguished by the violet shadows of masses of swollen cloud majestically rolling under the sun.

I was gazing with pleasure at this animated 'longshore picture, full of color and splendor and movement, when I observed a gentleman rapidly coming along the pier, which happened to be almost deserted. There was something of a deep-sea roll in his gait, and though he clutched a stick in one hand, the other hung down at his side in a manner that is peculiar to people who have long used the sea. I seemed to guess who he was, and watched him approaching while I knocked the ashes out of my pipe. He came to the edge of the wall, and, looking down, shouted out in a hoarse voice:

"Is this schooner the Casandra?"

"Yes, sir," I answered.

He put his hand on the ladder and descended. He had a clean-shaven face, the color of which at this moment was a fiery red, but then he had been walking fast. His eyes were large, and remarkable for an expression of eager expectation, as though he had been all his life waiting to receive some important communication. His hat was a broad-brimmed beaver; he was buttoned up in a stout bottle-green coat, and he was booted after the fashion of country gentlemen of that age.

"My name is Noble—Captain Noble," said he. "Are you Mr. Portlack?"

"I am," said I.

"Give me your hand," he exclaimed. He grasped and squeezed my fingers almost bloodless, letting go my hand with a vehement jerk as though he threw it from him. "I thank you for bringing my daughter home, sir. Her mother thanks you for your attention to her child. You have acted the part of a gentleman, of a sailor, of a man of honor. I thank you again, and yet again." Then, glancing along the decks of the vessel, he added, "So *this* is the blasted schooner, hey?"

"I trust Miss Noble has told you," said I, "how it happens that I was on board this vessel on the night of her abduction?"

"Yes," he answered, still continuing to examine the vessel curiously, now looking aloft, now forward, now aft, as though he could not take too complete a view of the craft. "Yes, she told me. The scoundrels! Thank God! I shot one of 'em. I would have shot 'em all, but the ruffians stood over me and my son with naked cutlasses and loaded pistols."

"I hope they did not burn the house down?"

"No, we extinguished the fire. Fifteen hundred pounds' worth of damage—that's all!" He made a cut through the air with his stick, exclaiming: "The rogues! the villains! They took me unaware. So many of them, too! How many were there?"

"Two Spaniards," said I, "the master of this

schooner, and four seamen. You were attacked by seven."

"Seven!" he cried. "Seven against two! for as to my coachman and footman—what do you think? They drove away—by heavens! they lashed the horses and bolted! I should like to go below; I should like to examine this blackguard craft. A fine, stout vessel all the same. A pirate in her day, no doubt."

We descended into the cabin, which he at once made the round of, peering at the pictures, staring at the looking-glasses, examining the chairs, as though he were in a museum and every object was extraordinarily curious.

"And pray, how is Miss Noble, sir?" said I. "I have not seen her since Tuesday."

"Very well; wonderfully well," he answered.

"How do you find her in looks after her terrible experience?"

"Why, neither her mother nor I see any change. She is a shade paler than she commonly is. But the girl has the heart of a lioness."

"So she has, sir."

"Now," said he, "Mr. Portlack, tell me about those two cursed Spaniards. I want to get at them."

He flung his stick upon the table and threw himself into an arm-chair.

"What did your daughter tell you about those two men?" said I.

"Why, she was insensible, she says, for the greater part of the time, and you informed her that, on the day of her recovery, you transshipped the two miscreants at their request. What vessel received them?" and here he pulled out a pocket-book and a pencil-case, with the intention of taking notes.

"Your daughter told you that she was insensible, sir, and that she continued insensible for many days?"

"Yes," said he, flourishing his pencil with an irritable gesture, clearly annoyed at my not answering *his* question.

"That," said I, "is all that she would be able to tell you."

My manner caused him to view me steadfastly, and the odd expression of expectation in his eyes grew more defined.

"When your daughter awoke from her first swoon, Captain Noble, she awoke—mad."

"What do you mean by mad?" he said.

"She was a maniac," said I. "And I wish that were all."

"Out with it—out with it *all*, then, man, for God's sake!" he exclaimed.

"Only one Spaniard, along with the Spanish steward, left the schooner. The body of the other Spaniard we dropped overboard."

He put his note-book on the table and tightly folded his arms on his breast. I believe, though I could not be sure, that he then guessed what I was about to tell him.

"I knew that your daughter was mad," said I. "Don Christoval introduced me into her cabin, hoping, I know not what, from my visit. It was not long after, that, being in the quarters which I then occupied yonder," said I, pointing, "I heard a terrible cry, and opening that door there I witnessed Don Christoval in the act of falling and expiring, stabbed to the heart by your daughter, who stood just within her cabin — that one there — grasping a large knife she had managed to get possession of."

He fell back in his chair, and remained for some moments looking at me as though he could not understand my meaning; then a sort of groan escaped him, and he got up and began to march about the cabin.

"These are dreadful tidings for a father's ears,"

he exclaimed, stopping abreast of me. Then his
mood changed with almost electric swiftness, and,
hitting the table a heavy blow with his fist, he
roared out: "By —, but it served the ruffian right!
It was *my* spirit working in her, mad as she might
be. That's how I would have served him, and the
rest of them, one and all—the atrocious villains!"

"Of course you know," said I, "that your
daughter is utterly ignorant of having slain that
Spaniard—ignorant of that, and ignorant that she
was out of her mind: though some dark fancy
seemed to haunt her for a while, until, by a falsehood, which I detest, I dispelled it."

"What did you tell her?"

"She asked me if she had been mad, and I said
'No'!"

"Mr. Portlack," he cried, grasping me by the
hand, "you have the delicacy of a gentleman. The
more I know of you the more I honor you. . . .
And she stabbed him to the heart? Oh, now,
to think of it! Her mother must not be told—
there must not be a whisper; she is all nerves and
imagination. Who knows of this beside yourself?"

"The five seamen," said I; "the five of a crew
of Englishmen, who, when they found that they had

been tricked by the Spaniards, resolved to leave the schooner. They sailed away in a boat for Cadiz when we were off that port. They know all about the assassination ; but, take my word for it, they'll never let you hear of them on this side of the grave."

He began to pace the cabin afresh.

"There is another," said I, "who possesses the secret, to call it so."

" You mean yourself?"

" No ; a lad—a negro boy. He is now in the schooner. I am troubled to know what to do with him. I have made him believe that he and I will both be hanged if he opens his lips. Yet, he may talk by and by, Captain Noble. He is a mere lad."

" What is to be done?" said he, frowning. " Tough as I am, it would break my heart if this were to be known. Conceive the effect of the intelligence upon my daughter. Great Heaven! if you could but tell me it was a dream of yours! Upon *your* secrecy, Mr. Portlack, I know we can all depend. Your behavior throughout is warrant enough for me. How to thank you— But about this boy? Let me see him, will you?"

I at once went on deck and called down into the forecastle, where the lad lay asleep in a bunk. I

18

told him to clean himself and come to me in the cabin, and I then returned to Captain Noble.

"There is only this lad to deal with," said I. "Believe me when I assure you that you will never hear more of those five seamen, nor of Don Lazarillo and the steward. Captain Dopping, the master of this schooner, you yourself shot dead. As for me— But for myself I will say no more than this: I hold that your daughter was barbarously used. The men who stole her, and who drove her mad by stealing her, were scoundrels whom I would have shot down as I would shoot down a brace of mad mongrels, sooner than have suffered them, as foreigners, to lay violent hands upon a countrywoman of mine, and upon so good and sweet a young lady as your daughter. My one desire throughout has been to make all the amends in my power. I was innocently betrayed into this villainous business, and I trust, Captain Noble, that the theory of reparation I have endeavored to work out establishes me in your mind as a man in whose keeping the tragic secret of this adventure is absolutely safe."

He endeavored to speak, but his voice failed him. He took my hand in both his, and in silence looked at me with his eyes dim with tears.

"And now about the boy," said I. "It occurs

to me that you might have influence to procure him some situation on board a man-of-war, going abroad or at present abroad."

He was about to answer, when the lad's legs showed in the companion-way and down he came. Captain Noble stared at him, and he stared at the Captain.

"A likely lad, Mr. Portlack. Does he speak English?"

"Do you speak English, Tom?" said I.

"Nuffin but English, de Lord be praised!" he answered, grinning.

Captain Noble mused as he eyed him. "You have behaved very honestly," said he, "and I shall want to do you a kindness. Come to the hotel where I am stopping to-morrow morning at ten o'clock, and you and I will have a chat."

"I'll be dere, sah."

"It will give me time to think," said Captain Noble in an aside to me. "And come you and dine with us this evening, Mr. Portlack, will you?" I glanced down at my clothes. "Never mind about your dress," he continued. "We shall expect you at half-past six o'clock."

He stayed for another quarter of an hour, and then left the schooner.

Never had anything before, and I may say never has anything since, proved so memorable to me as that dinner with Captain and Lady Ida Noble and Miss Noble at the Albion Hotel, Ramsgate. The reason why it was memorable you shall hear in a minute. I found Lady Ida Noble very different from the individual I had supposed her to be, on the representations of Don Christoval. I expected to meet a tall, haughty, and forbidding lady, of an ice-like coldness of demeanor; instead, I found her an impulsive little woman, in a high degree nervous and emotional, possessed of a ready capacity of tears, resembling her daughter in face and figure in a sort of miniature way—for Miss Noble stood half a head taller than her mother—and a refined lady in all she said and did. She overwhelmed me with thanks, and seemed unable to make enough of me.

Miss Noble looked very well indeed; there was color in her cheek and fire in her soft dark eyes, and a quiet vivacity of good health in her bearing and movements. Indeed, her swift recovery, or rather, let me say, her emergence into health from the horrible disease of insanity and from her long death-like condition of catalepsy, impressed me then, as it impresses me still, as the most startling and extraordinary of all the incidents of our startling and extraordinary voyage.

When the ladies had left us, Captain Noble put a cigar-case upon the table, and said:

" I have been thinking about that negro boy. I have a relative in the West Indies, and I will send the lad out to him, if he is willing to go. I will tell my relative the story of my daughter's abduction, explain that I want the matter kept secret, and bid him have an eye to the lad."

" He is a good boy," said I, " and deserves a comfortable berth."

" He shall have it," said Captain Noble, " and I will put money in his pocket, too. I'll talk with him in the morning."

He then questioned me about Don Lazarillo, but I could tell him nothing. The very name, indeed, I said, might be assumed, though I thought this improbable, seeing that the other had sailed under true colors. In talking of these Spaniards he, by design or accident, informed me that his daughter was heiress to a considerable property. I can not be sure of the amount he named, but I have a recollection of his saying that on her mother's death she would inherit a fortune of between sixty thousand and eighty thousand pounds. One subject leading to another, he inquired as to the payment of the sailors of La Casandra. I answered that Don Lazarillo, being terrified by the seamen's threats, had entered his dead friend's berth and produced a bag of gold which exactly sufficed to discharge the claims of the men.

"And what did the rogues offer you, Mr. Portlack?" said he.

"Fifty guineas, sir."

"Did you get it?"

I smiled, and answered that, instead of money, Don Lazarillo had given me Don Christoval's watch and chain and diamond ring.

"Have you the things upon you?" said he.

"I have the ring," said I, pulling it out of my waistcoat pocket. "The watch and chain I pawned for twenty pounds, being without money, save a trifle in a savings bank in London. What this ring is worth I'm sure I can't imagine," said I, looking at it. "I hope it will yield me an outfit. I as good as lost everything I possessed when the Ocean Ranger sailed away in chase of the Yankee, leaving me adrift."

He extended his hand for the ring, and appeared to examine it. "Have you the pawn-ticket for the watch and chain?" he asked. I gave it to him.

"I should like to possess that watch and chain," said he, "and I should like also to possess this ring. I'll buy them from you."

I bowed, scarcely as yet seeing my way. He pulled out his pocket-book and extracted a check already filled in.

"You will do me the favor," said he, "to accept this as a gift, and I will do you the favor to accept this pawn-ticket and ring as a gift."

The check was for five hundred guineas.

This noble check is the reason for my calling that dinner at the Albion Hotel, Ramsgate, a memorable one. It laid the foundations of the little fortune which I now possess, but which without that check I should never have possessed, so hopelessly unprofitable is the vocation of the mariner. But I did even better than that out of the ill-fated Don Christoval and his friend, for, nobody appearing to claim the schooner, she was sold after a considerable lapse of time; and when I returned from a voyage in which I had gone as chief officer, I was agreeably surprised at being informed, by the solicitor whom I had requested to watch my interests during my absence, that the claim he had made on my behalf as virtually the salvor of the schooner had been admitted, and that I was the richer by a proportion of the proceeds amounting to a hundred and ninety pounds.

Whether because of the influence possessed by Captain Noble, or because the authorities (whoever *they* might be) decided not to take proceedings against me as the only discoverable member of the gang who had forced Miss Noble from her home, certain it is that I never heard anything more of the matter. I took care that my address should be known, and carefully informed the receiver at Ramsgate, and Captain Noble also, that I was willing while ashore at any moment to come forward and state what I knew; but, as I have before said, I was never communicated with. The whole story lay as dead in the minds of those few who knew of it as though the events I have related had never occurred.

Five years had expired since the date of my having safely restored Miss Noble to her parents.

I was now commanding a large Australian passenger ship, and among those who sailed to Melbourne with me was a gentleman named Fairfield. He was a solicitor in practice at Carlisle. One day, in conversing with him, by the merest accident I happened to pronounce the name of Captain Noble. He asked me if I knew him. I answered warily that I had heard of him. He grew garrulous—an unusual weakness in a lawyer—and, in the course of a long quarter-deck yarn, told me that Miss Noble had been for two years out of her mind, tended as a lunatic by nurses in her father's house, but for nearly two years now she had been perfectly well, and some six months ago had married Sir Ralph A——, Bart., a widower, whose estate lay within five miles of her father's. He said that there was some mystery about the lady's past. She had been abducted and ill-used. He never could get at the truth himself, and would like to learn it. He understood that she went out of her mind because of some horrible haunting fancy of having committed a murder.

That was all he could tell me, and from that day to this I have never been able to hear of either her or her people.

THE END.